BACK TO SPELL ONE

WESTERN WOODS MYSTERY #1

SAMANTHA SILVER

BLUEBERRY BOOKS PRESS

CHAPTER 1

Seattle in the summer was absolutely gorgeous. Not too hot, not too cold, with the warm sun beating down on me, making my walk to my absolutely hellish job just a little bit more tolerable.

It was all going to be worth it, I kept telling myself. I mean sure, working behind the bar in an upscale club in downtown Seattle definitely had its downsides. There were the frat boys who thought they were God's gift to women, and the creepy old guys in suits who figured they could buy their way into my pants, the drunks who didn't understand the meaning of the words "you've had enough for one night" and everything else in between. But hey, the money was good. The money was *very* good, in fact, for someone like me who had absolutely no education outside of my high school diploma, and who was trying to save up some money to go to college. I hadn't quite figured out what

I was going to study yet. Maybe I'd go into nursing? That seemed like the sort of thing I'd be good at.

But for now, I was going to go through another eight-hour shift in the job I hated, in the hopes that someday – hopefully in the next year or so – I'd have saved up enough money that I could go to college, even if it was only part-time, and start building a real career.

After all, I was now twenty-six years old, and it was time to start thinking about what I was really going to do with my life. I wasn't going to be able to tend bar forever, after all. And I most certainly didn't want to.

I made my way to the club, in the trendy Seattle neighborhood of Belltown. Passing through the large red door that made the club I worked at instantly recognizable – it was called Red Door, after all – I headed towards the bar where Jake, one of my coworkers, was already at the till counting the cash for the night.

"Way to show up on time, White," he said without looking up.

Did I mention I hated my job yet?

"My shift starts at seven, and it's six fifty-seven," I muttered in reply.

"Well, I've been here for fifteen minutes already, getting everything set for when we open."

"Congratulations on giving away your labor for free, then. I believe in being paid when I'm here."

"Whatever. Can you go downstairs and grab another case of Jack Daniels? We're basically out."

I stuffed my purse under the counter and nodded. "Sure."

I made my way towards a black door at the back of the room with 'staff only' stenciled in red letters. Passing through it, I ran into Lisa, one of the managers of the club. Lisa was probably the only person here I actually liked; she understood that this job was a stepping stone for me and that the club business wasn't really something I wanted to be a part of long-term.

"Hey, Tina," she greeted me with a warm smile. "How are you?"

"Good, thanks," I replied. "You?"

"Super busy! Apparently, K-Team's bachelor party is coming here tonight."

I rolled my eyes. "Great, that's what we need."

"Well, the publicity will be great, at least. See ya!"

K-Team was the name of the Instagram account of a local "celebrity". He had over a million followers on Instagram, and his whole account was basically based around being as big of a douche as possible – posing with fast cars while wearing sunglasses, showing off his money, working out, all that sort of thing.

I mean, I knew I probably shouldn't judge without seeing them, but I had a feeling K-Team's bachelor party crew weren't exactly going to be a group of well-behaved, model citizens that were going to make my life easy tonight.

Making my way downstairs, where we stored the extra alcohol, I stepped around cases of beer until I found the extra bottles of Jack. To be honest, I didn't really mind this part of the job. It took ages for me to lug cases back up the stairs, but I always felt like it was basically a workout I was getting paid to do. Plus, when I finally managed to get a case from downstairs and back to the bar, I always felt a cool sense of accomplishment. I was basically Wonder Woman, right?

I settled into the routine of daily life as the doors to the club opened and revelers began to make their way in. We opened at nine, but generally things didn't really start to get going until around eleven, and then we had three hours of chaos until two, when we closed up for the night.

I had to admit, things had actually been going pretty well up until around midnight. Two bachelorette parties had come in, and while they were all definitely drunk, they were polite about it, and one of the girls even gave me a $100 tip on behalf of one of the brides.

Then, around midnight, K-Team and his entourage came in, and everything changed. As he came towards the bar, I had to stop from laughing. The guy was maybe five eight, with his hair slicked back like he was Scott Caan or something, wearing so many gold chains it was a miracle he managed to hold his head up. He wore a blazer over a pair of low-cut jeans and a white t-shirt, and still had his Ray Bans on, even though we were not only indoors, but in a super-dark club.

As he swaggered through the crowd – there was

really no other way to describe the way he was walking – his entourage pushed anyone who got too close away. There had to be fifteen guys with him, all surrounding K-Team like he was some kind of God.

"Great, this is going to be just awesome," Jake muttered under his breath, and for once, I agreed with him. There was no way K-Town and his team weren't going to be absolutely awful customers.

"Yo, bartender," K-Town announced when we made his way to the bar. "The crew and I need some bubbly. Ten bottles of your best," he ordered, slapping a credit card down on the table.

I waited until I faced the bar, getting ready to grab some of the bottles he had ordered before rolling my eyes.

"We're going to be at the table at the back. Make sure hottie over there brings us the bottles," K-Town said, pointing towards me. My face grew red. It wasn't anything I hadn't heard before, but I still wasn't entirely used to it. My parents – a wonderful couple who couldn't have children of their own and adopted me when I was a toddler – had always taught me to be respectful of other people and their bodies. It wasn't until I worked here that I realized just how many people could have used parents that were more like mine.

Their entourage spent the entire night making disparaging comments about my body, and by the time we closed at two, I was almost in tears. I knew I had to be stronger than this. I knew this was the real world, and that comments like that were the norm, but I had to admit, it still hurt. I wasn't the outgoing, popular girl in high school. I had never been the type to go out to clubs and parties and that sort of thing. I wasn't really used to being around drunk people who were a bit looser with their lips – and their hands – than they might have been while sober, and K-Team and his entourage were the worst customers I'd had in a long time in that regard.

When I finally cashed out and grabbed my stuff, just before three in the morning, Jake looked at me with something other than hatred in his eyes for the first time. "Yo, you want me to drive you home or something? Those guys were bad, tonight."

I shook my head no. "Thanks. I'm just going to walk. I only live about ten blocks away."

"Cool."

I just wanted to get home, have a long, hot shower, crawl under the covers and sleep away the awfulness of tonight. I wanted to forget about the comments about my body. I wanted to forget about the leering stares.

I really, really wished I had enough money to enroll into college now.

As I left the club, I let out a sigh of relief. It always felt good to feel the cool night air on my face after hours in the stuffy club full of sweaty people grinding against one another. Plus, the feeling of the air on my face was the ultimate symbol of my freedom. I now had sixteen hours before I had to be there again for my next shift. Sixteen hours to sleep, watch Netflix, maybe read some of the latest book I was working through, *Big Little Lies.*

I started walking away from the club and back towards home. It was just a short walk to the tiny studio apartment I'd been lucky enough to rent for below market rates for the simple reason that I was pretty sure it broke every single rule in the fire code. But hey, I couldn't afford Seattle prices otherwise, and certainly not downtown, so who was I to complain? At least I didn't have any roommates.

"Hey, you," I suddenly heard behind me. My blood went cold. I turned and saw K-Team. He was by himself now, his gold chains twinkling under the streetlight. "Come over here."

"No, thanks, I'm heading home," I replied. A million thoughts ran through my head. Should I try and go back to the club? No, K-Town was between me and the club; I'd have to get past him to get back there. I was still about eight blocks from home. Could I outrun him? Those chains had to weigh a ton, and while he spent so much time at the gym, he obviously regularly skipped leg day.

"Aw, but honey, I told all my crew to bail so we could have some alone time," he said, taking a couple of steps towards me. I wanted to vomit. Was this really happening?

"Leave me alone," I said, clutching my purse closer

to my body and taking a step backwards. "I don't want to hang out with you."

"Come on, sweetie. It's my bachelor night. I'm allowed to have a bit of fun, aren't I?"

This was not good.

CHAPTER 2

There was definitely no more time to try and figure things out. I had a feeling my words weren't going to have any kind of effect on K-Team. If I tried to run past him and get back to the club he might grab me, so I did the next best thing: I turned and ran away, hoping to get home first, or to find someone to help me.

As I darted down the street, I became all too aware of one thing: I definitely needed to hit the gym a little bit more. I instantly began panting and sweating, but none of that mattered, because I had to get as far away from this disgusting creep as possible. I didn't even want to think about what he had planned.

"Hey, wait," he called out after me, but I didn't stop. I didn't even turn to see if he was coming after me. I thought I could hear footsteps behind me, but I didn't know for sure. I didn't dare turn to look.

My brown hair whipped into my face as I ran, and I wished I'd thought to put it in a ponytail tonight. I couldn't really see where I was going, and while I knew the route I needed to take, it was dark, I was panicking, and it just wasn't really a great situation all around.

I was only about three blocks from home when I stumbled on the pavement and launched towards one of the trees that lined Bell Street. Who knew that Seattle's green space was going to be what eventually took me out?

A cry of surprise escaped my lips, and I closed my eyes, bracing for impact as I pitched head-first towards the tree. To my surprise, however, I found myself hitting the ground, my hands and knees scraping against grass rather than my face meeting the bark of the tree.

"What the-" I started, opening my eyes and looking around. This was way too weird.

Instead of being in downtown Seattle, I looked to be at the entrance of a forest. Behind me was a single huge oak tree, surrounded on either side by about 50 yards of grass, with a single woodchip path leading into a large forest of coniferous trees.

Where on earth was I? I had lived in Seattle my entire life; this was definitely nowhere near the city.

"Well, hello there, I see you've had a bit of an adventure coming back through Eddie," a man's voice said from behind me.

I gasped as I stood up and looked to see where the

voice was coming from. The man behind me was at least six foot two, with long, blonde hair and dazzling blue eyes that reminded me suspiciously of the Ice Walkers from *Game of Thrones.*

"Who are you?" I asked, stepping away from the man.

"I was about to ask you the same thing," the man replied, making his way towards me. "I've never seen you come to Western Woods before."

"Western Woods?"

"Why yes, of course. Eddie here is the portal tree between the Western Woods and the human world."

"The human world? What is this? Some sort of trick? Some sort of weird *Alice in Wonderland* kind of thing?"

"What is *Alice in Wonderland*?"

"Am I dead?" I was starting to seriously consider the possibility that this was what had happened. Was this heaven? Or, whatever the afterlife was? Had I maybe hit my head on the tree, and that was it for me? Right now, I had absolutely no idea.

"I must say, you're acting rather strangely for a paranormal. What kind are you?"

"I'm not a paranormal at all," I replied. "I'm just a normal person, from Seattle, and I was just trying to get home after escaping a creepy guy, when I tripped and fell into a tree. Have I died? You certainly don't look like how I imagined Saint Peter would look."

Saint Peter had never been painted with abs and

muscles that bulged against his shirt when I was in church.

"You can't be a normal person," the man replied. "The portal only works if you have paranormal powers."

"Well, I don't. I don't know what these paranormal powers you're talking about are. But so, I'm not dead?"

The man laughed. "Of course you're not dead. Well, at least, I don't think you are. You certainly don't have the teeth of the vampire, and you're completely opaque so you're not a ghost, although I suppose vampires are undead rather than dead. No, I believe you're very much alive. The question is, what are you? Shifter? You certainly don't look like any I've ever seen. No, I think you're more likely to be a witch."

"A witch?" I asked. "No. No, none of this can be real. Witches don't exist, vampires don't exist, and I don't even know what a shifter is."

The man grinned at me. "You really have no idea what a shifter is?"

I shook my head. *That* was what he took from my last sentence?

I gasped in surprise as all of a sudden the man was covered in a blinding light; it was so bright that I covered my eyes until a second later it disappeared, and the man was replaced instead with a huge, terrifying dragon. He had the same blue eyes as the man, and scales that glittered in a combination of yellow, orange, and red.

My mouth dropped open. "This cannot be real," I repeated, shaking my head. Nope. Dragons didn't exist. They just didn't. And where on earth had that man gone? Surely, he couldn't have turned into the dragon. It just wasn't possible.

And yet, I could actually see the resemblance. The eyes were the same, and the shades of the scales looked a lot like the man's blond hair. A second later, the dragon began to warp; he became smaller and smaller and eventually had turned back into the man. Had that seriously just happened?

"Now you know what a shifter is," the man said with a grin. I was pretty sure my mouth was permanently dropped open. "So tell me, what magical town do you come from that you've never heard of shifters? I've met a lot of travelers in my time, and a lot of different paranormals, and every single one of them has known what a shifter is. Where do you come from?"

"I'm from Seattle," I finally managed to stammer out.

"No, no. What paranormal town are you from?"

"I'm not from a paranormal town. I'm telling you, I'm from Seattle."

The man tilted his head towards me, and for the first time, I had a feeling he thought I was telling the truth.

"Interesting. So you've never been to the paranormal world?"

I shook my head no.

"Well, it's impossible for you to have passed through Eddie if you didn't have paranormal powers. I suppose I'll have to take you into town and sort this out."

"Into town?" I asked. The man motioned to the path that led into the forest.

"It's only about a quarter mile away. We can easily walk there."

I definitely didn't want to follow this strange man into a forest, and this weird world, when I had absolutely no idea what was going on. But I didn't really know what other options I had. The man began to stride off along the path, and I followed after him.

"What's your name, anyway?" I asked as I jogged up behind him.

"I am Drake," the man answered. "And you?"

"Tina," I replied. As we entered the forest, I was a little bit worried about the light situation. After all, traveling in the dark without any light hadn't gone very well for me tonight. I pulled out my phone, to turn on the flashlight, but as soon as we crossed the threshold into the forest a million dancing lights suddenly appeared out of nowhere.

I gasped as the lights danced around, giving us more than enough light to see where we were going.

"What are they?" I asked, my curiosity overtaking my fear.

"They are called Hotaru," Drake replied. "They are creatures of love, and givers of light."

I watched in awe as the Hotaru followed us along the path, until finally the trees broke and revealed the most gorgeous town I had ever seen.

"Is this... What did you say this place was called?" I asked Drake.

"Western Woods," Drake replied. "Yes, this is the town."

Western Woods looked exactly like I would have imagined a cute Alpine village in Germany to be. The buildings all had thatched roofs, half-timbered buildings and huge shutters surrounding the windows with plants growing from them. The streets were all cobblestone-lined, and I didn't see a car in sight. Maybe that was just because it was the middle of the night, though.

To our left ran a small, slow-flowing river, lined with Gothic railings. French-style streetlights cast a warm glow on everything, and I couldn't help but notice that there were no actual bulbs or flame inside the lights. It appeared the light was actually formed by magic.

But that couldn't be possible. Magic wasn't real. At least, I was pretty sure it wasn't. The more time I spent here, the more I felt like I didn't know anything.

CHAPTER 3

"Where are we going?" I asked Drake as we made our way down the cobbled streets.

"I'm taking you to see the Chief Enforcer," Drake replied. "As we don't know what kind of paranormal you are, I figure that is the safest route to take."

"Chief Enforcer, is that like, the police?"

"I do not know what this police is that you speak of, but the Chief Enforcer is in charge of ensuring that all paranormals follow the laws and rules of our land."

"Okay, that does sound like our police."

After a couple of minutes we arrived in front of a large, stone building. It had been whitewashed, with large turrets with a cute orange roof. If I hadn't known any better, I would have assumed it was some sort of Gothic church.

Drake led me through the large wooden doors at

the front, and we found ourselves in a huge expanse of place, the walls and ceiling all made of dark wood. Tapestries covered the walls, and I was so enthralled by the sight of this wonder that I forgot to be scared for a minute.

"Drake," an authoritative female voice said a moment later, the sound echoing through the large space. "What brings you here at this hour in the morning?"

I looked up to see a tall, slender woman with long, wavy blonde hair that nearly reached her hips make her way towards us. Her eyes were dark, but not unfriendly. Dressed in a dark suit, she definitely looked professional. Her eyes found mine, and she looked me up and down, as though judging me.

"Chief Enforcer King, I'm afraid I have a bit of a situation. Could we go into your office?"

The woman led us to a room off to the side, which was much smaller, but still decorated in the same mahogany wood. A framed certificate against the far wall was the only decoration in the room, and the window behind the Chief Enforcer's desk looked out over the river. She motioned for the two of us to sit down in comfortable -looking chairs in front of her desk, waiting for us to be seated before sitting in hers.

"What's going on?" she asked Drake.

"This, uh, human found her way through Eddie," Drake replied, motioning towards me.

"That's impossible," the woman replied. "I had Lita

herself set the spell. There is no way anyone who doesn't have paranormal powers can get through there."

"I know," Drake agreed, nodding. "However, whatever powers this woman may have, she has no idea what they are."

The woman turned to face me. I gulped hard; those dark eyes were quite intimidating.

"Who are you?"

"Tina White," I answered, swallowing hard. My mouth felt super dry all of a sudden.

"And where are you from? Are you a witch?"

I shook my head. "No, I'm not. I'm from Seattle, in what Drake keeps referring to as the human world."

"Who are your parents? You say your name is White, I have never heard that name."

"My parents were Nancy and Carl White. They adopted me when I was a baby. No one knows who my real parents were; I was abandoned in front of the hospital when I was only a few weeks old. Or at least, that's what I've been told. My parents - Nancy and Carl - both died. Dad passed away from cancer when I was 12, and mom had a heart attack last year."

Chief Enforcer King and Drake shared a look.

"So you have no idea who your biological parents are?" the Chief Enforcer asked. I shook my head.

"No. None at all."

"Explain to me exactly how you came to Western Woods," Chief Enforcer King ordered. I told her all about my night, and how K-Town had found me after my shift and I had run to escape him before tripping into the tree.

"Well, if one thing is certain here, it is that you have magical powers of some sort."

"But how? How did I go so long without knowing?"

"You would have had to have a wand," Chief Enforcer King replied. "I believe you are a witch, although in the morning I will get the coven head to tell us for sure. Unfortunately, that sort of magic is beyond my scope."

Despite the fact that Chief Enforcer King was incredibly intimidating, I couldn't help but ask the question which was now plaguing me. "What kind of paranormal are you? Do you change into a dragon, like Drake?"

Chief Enforcer King smiled at me. "I'm a lion shifter," she told me.

My mouth dropped open. "So you can like, change into a lion at will?"

She nodded. "Yes, I can. You really have had no experience with the paranormal world, have you?"

I shook my head.

"Well, we're going to have to change that for you. Since it's the middle of the night, I don't want to interrupt anyone else. We have a small room in this building that is generally used by Enforcers if they need to take a break during their shifts. It has a bed, and a shower. You're welcome to use them tonight if you'd like."

"Thank you," I said. "To be honest, I'm exhausted, and that sounds really nice right now."

"Thank you for bringing Tina to me," Chief Enforcer King said to Drake. "You're welcome to resume your post at the portal now."

Drake nodded and stood up, shooting me a quick comforting smile before leaving the room.

Chief Enforcer King stood up a minute after Drake had left the room, and motioned for me to follow her. When we left her office, she led me to the far end of the main hall, and into a smaller room at the back of the building. Sure enough, it was a small room with a single bed in the corner, and a bathroom off to the right.

"Feel free to spend the rest of the night here," Chief Enforcer King said. "I will come and get you in the morning, when I have had the opportunity to speak with the head of the coven."

I nodded, thanking her, and as soon as she left I made my way into the bathroom and had a hot shower. I slipped under the covers, wondering what on earth I had gotten myself into. Maybe this was all just a dream, and as soon as I fell asleep in this dream, I would wake back up in my bed in my studio apartment in Seattle.

Despite the craziness of the night, the exhaustion that wracked my body quickly overtook me, and I fell asleep almost as soon as my head hit the pillow.

CHAPTER 4

I woke up the next morning to the sound of rapping on the wooden door leading to my room.

"Come in," I called out, jumping out of bed. It took me a second to realize exactly where I was, as the events of the previous night came flooding back to me. It hadn't been a dream after all. I was really sitting here, in the middle of some sort of magical town. The woman knocking on the door was in all likelihood the chief of police here, who could change into a lion at will.

The door opened a second later, and sure enough, Chief Enforcer King made her way in.

"How did you sleep?" she asked.

"Pretty well, but I sure could use a few more hours."

"I thought so, so I brought you something from The

Hexpresso Bean. It's the local coffee shop here in town."

I reached for the coffee gratefully, the warm aroma of roasted beans instantly making me feel more awake. To my surprise, the coffee was topped with whipped cream and sprinkles, and it looked like there was a copious amount of syrup that had been poured down the side of the cup. I sipped at the drink, and as the creamy coffee made its way down my throat, I suddenly felt so much more refreshed, like I'd had a full night's sleep. Something about this was weird. Coffee was amazing, after all, but it wasn't normally anything like this. This was like, well, coffee on steroids.

"Is there magic involved in this coffee?" I asked, not quite knowing how to phrase my question properly.

Chief Enforcer King smiled. "Yes. That's the beauty of the product from The Hexpresso Bean. They add a shot of a certain potion to all of the coffees, so that whatever you need, the coffee gives it to you. If you haven't gotten any sleep, it gives you energy to get you through the day, without the caffeine crash. If you're nervous about something at work, it will lessen your anxiety."

I stared at the cup, not entirely sure how I felt about this. Caffeine was one thing, magic was another entirely. "So I just drank some sort of strange magic potion?" I asked.

"Don't worry," Chief Enforcer King told me. "You'll get used to it. Magic is a part of your life now. And speaking of, we have to go and see the head of the coven."

I stood up and followed wordlessly after her as we made our way out of the small room and into the main part of the building. As we left the building and I got my first glimpse of Western Woods during the day, I had to admit, I was incredibly impressed.

The sun shone down upon the town, and now, there were other people milling around in the streets.

A tall, graceful woman with pointed ears that I was pretty sure was an elf, smiled curiously at us as we passed her. I had to make a conscious effort not to stare. Elves were real too? And when we passed by a cute woman floating in the air, a pair of golden wings fluttering at a million miles an hour behind her, that was just too much. My mouth dropped open and I stopped to look.

"She's a fairy," Chief Enforcer King told me.

"No way," I almost whispered. "That's crazy."

"Come, you don't want to keep the head of the coven waiting."

Chief Enforcer King led me towards a whitewashed brick building with a green-domed top. It was about the size of a large house, and as soon as we got to the front door, Chief Enforcer King knocked.

A moment later the door opened, and a girl about my age with a black pixie haircut and round black eyes looked out at us.

"Chief Enforcer King," the woman said. "What a wonderful surprise."

"Hello, Amy," Chief Enforcer King replied. "I called Lita a couple of hours ago; I need to speak with her."

"Of course," Amy replied, opening the door wide and leading us through. She looked at me, her eyes full of curiosity.

"Hi, I'm Tina," I said to her, holding out a hand.

"Amy," the witch replied. "Which coven are you from? Normally, I can tell, but I don't recognize you."

Before I had a chance to answer, Chief Enforcer King interrupted. "I'm sure there will be plenty of time for chatting later, but for now we need to see the head of the coven."

Amy nodded quickly, obviously embarrassed at having been chastised. "Of course, Chief Enforcer King. I'm so sorry. Please, follow me."

The three of us made our way down a hallway lined with plush, scarlet-red carpeting. At the very end of the hall was a set of gold-gilded doors so ornate I stopped to have a look at them for a second before Amy threw them open.

"Miss Sahera, I have Chief Enforcer King, and, uh, Tina to see you," she announced pompously, before closing the door behind us.

I wasn't sure what I had expected the leader of a coven to look like. After all, it wasn't like I had a lot of experience with witches, what with having assumed they weren't real for my entire life. Was a coven leader going to be old, with warts on her long nose and a crackling laugh? Or maybe she would be more like Professor McGonagall from *Harry Potter*, stern but fair.

In reality, though, the leader of the coven was nothing like either. When I had been in elementary school, my best friend was Kirsten Rosetti. Her mother, bless her, was the most amazing woman. She was always bustling around, always telling us we weren't eating enough, always encouraging, always the friendliest of all the mothers. But, if Kirsten ever did anything bad, my goodness did she ever have a temper.

Miss Sahera reminded me exactly of Kirsten's mom.

"Welcome, welcome. Aria, please, come on in and have a seat. And Tina! It's so lovely to meet you," Miss Sahera said, making her way towards me with her arms outstretched. She was rather on the hefty side, with curly black hair that framed her friendly face. She took me into a huge hug, and I had trouble breathing. Miss Sahera was definitely stronger than she looked.

"Welcome to the magical world, my dear. Aria here tells me you're likely a witch, but one with no idea as to her powers. Now, I can't tell you the transition will be easy – frankly I've never known anyone in your particular situation – but let me tell you I will do my best to make sure you know exactly what it means to be a witch and that you're brought up to speed as quickly as possible. Now, to start with, we're going to need to get you a wand."

Chief Enforcer King coughed. "I'm sorry, Lita, but I

think first we need to determine for sure that she is a witch."

"Oh, of course she's a witch," Miss Sahera replied. "I can feel it in my bones. But if it makes you feel any better, I can do the spell."

"It would make me feel better," Chief Enforcer King replied. It was obvious that she wasn't a huge fan of Miss Sahera's rather lax style.

The witch in front of me took a wand out from her waistband. It was about a foot long, smooth and beige, with gold filament wrapped around it. About one third of the way up was a large pearl in the center of the wand, set in place with more gold. I gasped at just how incredible it looked.

She pointed the wand at me and closed her eyes. "*By the power of Jupiter, tell me is there witchcraft in her?*"

The tip of the wand suddenly glowed gold, and Miss Sahera gave a short nod.

"There we go. Confirmation that Tina here is a witch. You can leave her here with me. I'll alert the heads of the other clans. After all, I believe this situation is quite unnatural."

"Absolutely," Chief Enforcer King replied. "You'll be surprised at the questions she asks."

"Sorry," I said, a blush crawling up my face. "I hope it wasn't rude to ask you what kind of, uh, paranormal you were."

Chief Enforcer King smiled. "Not at all. I've simply never been asked the question before." It was true that after knowing the truth, she did have a rather lion-like look to her. I hoped that I was going to get better at recognizing people without having to ask awkward questions in the future. With that, Chief Enforcer King made her way back towards the doors, which opened for her automatically as she approached. I had a sneaking suspicion it wasn't the same technology that grocery stores used.

So it was official. I was a witch. I turned to Miss Sahera. I had a *lot* of questions.

CHAPTER 5

"*M*iss Sahera?" I started.

"Please, call me Lita. Everyone else does."

"Lita, I have some questions."

"I'm sure you do, dear. Please, have a seat," she said, motioning to what looked like a clear, pink exercise ball in the corner. I sat down on it gingerly, and to my surprise, the ball conformed to my body perfectly, and stayed in place. It was insanely comfortable, a bit like relaxing in a hammock. Lita sat down on the edge of her desk and looked at me curiously.

"I do wonder which coven you belong to. I'm certain we'll discover eventually which celestial power you're most attracted to. But please, ask away."

"So, um, how does being a witch work?" I asked. "I know you just did a spell, but how?"

"Oh my, you really have no knowledge of witchcraft. Now, witches are born into a certain coven. Magical powers are passed down through the female lineage, so as long as your mother was a witch, you were guaranteed to be a witch as well, regardless of your father's paranormal status. Your coven is the same as that of your mother's. Witches from a number of different families belong to the same coven, what connects a coven is the celestial object that powers our witchcraft."

"Yours is Jupiter?" I asked, remembering the spell Lita had cast.

She nodded. "Yes, we are a coven guided by Jupiter, the planet of storms. Our powers are at their strongest when thunder is around."

"And my coven is different?"

"In all likelihood, yes. As far as I'm aware, there were no secret pregnancies in this coven around twenty-five years ago."

"So how will we find out what coven I belong to? Like, what powers I have?"

"There is no way to know, except through experimentation. Once we discover where your powers come from, we should be able to contact the coven to which you truly belong, and we should be able to determine where you come from. We may even be able to determine who your real parents were."

That last sentence was like a punch to the chest. I'd spent my entire life having accepted the fact that there was no way I would ever know who my biological parents were. And now, not only had I just discovered that I was a witch with magical powers, but also that there was a chance that I could find out where I came from after all? Yeah, this was a lot to take in all at once.

"So there are other covens? Are they here in Western Woods as well?"

Lita smiled. "There are dozens of covens, yes. However, they generally live in other magical towns. Most magical towns where witches live are dominated by a single coven, although in some of the larger towns, two, and sometimes three covens all live together."

"Wait, there are more magical places that just here?"

"Of course. There are hundreds of magical towns located around the world. Each has its own unique residents, however, paranormals are allowed to travel freely between each. There are access points to each in both the human world, and in other paranormal towns."

This was totally crazy. It was going to take a while to get used to this, for sure.

"So, how am I going to learn to be a witch?" I asked. "I mean, you did that cool spell, but I don't know any of those sorts of things."

Lita frowned slightly. "That is going to be the biggest challenge here, I think. We have a coven school, of course. But it's designed for small children. Witches generally complete their formal education by the time they turn fourteen. There are advanced magical instruction courses for those looking to go into a career that involves more complex magical skills, but of course, you're nowhere near the level to be accepted into those. And quite frankly, I don't think anyone involved would enjoy you joining the class of four-year-olds to learn basic magic. However, I have an idea."

Lita pointed her wand towards the door, which shone a forest green color for a split second before Amy opened it.

"Yes?" she asked politely.

"Amy, would you mind coming in here for a second? I have something to ask you."

Amy did as she was asked, giving me a small smile as she made her way over and stood at attention in front of us.

"I have something to ask you," Lita said. "Tina here has absolutely no experience with magic whatsoever. I obviously don't want her joining the four-year-olds learning to use their magic for the first time, and I was wondering if you – perhaps with the help of the other girls your age – would be willing to bring Tina up to speed in your spare time."

Amy's dark eyes shimmered with excitement; despite her serious demeanor she couldn't quite keep the excitement off her face.

"Really? You want me to teach a complete beginner how to do magic?"

"Yes," Lita said with a smile. "You're a very talented witch, and I think you would be best suited to teach

Tina. Perhaps with the help of some of the other girls?"

"Of course, I would love to," Amy gushed. "Tina can come and live in our home, as well. We have that spare bedroom, after all, ever since Anastasia left."

"Good," Lita nodded. "So that's settled. Let me have a little bit more of a chat with Tina, and when we're done here I'll leave her with you."

I gave Amy a shy smile, and she practically grinned back at me. She could obviously barely contain her excitement as she nodded and left the room.

Lita gave me a kind smile when the door closed behind her once more. "Amy is one of our most naturally talented witches. She can be a little bit intense, but I trust that she and the other witches she lives with will be able to teach you properly."

"Thanks," I said quietly.

"I know this must all be a lot to take in," Lita said kindly. "I can't imagine how you must be feeling right now. Why don't I leave you with Amy, and you can try to get settled in?"

I nodded. "Sure."

"If you have any things you need from the human world, you can go back and get them in the morning."

"I don't really have much," I said softly. It was true. There were some pictures of my parents that I would treasure forever, but other than that, to be honest, I didn't really have all that much back in Seattle. After all, I saved all of my money so I could go to college.

Did this witch town have college?

Lita stood up and I followed after her as we made our way to the door. "Please, come by anytime if you need anything. I'm the head of the coven. I'm here to help you, even if strictly speaking you're not necessarily from *our* coven. But you're a witch, and we're going to take care of you."

"Thanks," I managed, giving Lita a smile. This was still very, *very* overwhelming.

As we passed out into the main hall once more, I noticed Chief Enforcer King was back. Her face was lined with worry.

"Chief Enforcer King needs to speak with you urgently," Amy said to the coven leader.

"Of course," Lita replied with a curt nod.

"There's nothing wrong with me being here, is there?" I asked, worried that the Chief's arrival here had something to do with me.

"No, don't worry," King told me. "This new development has nothing to do with you."

"Amy, feel free to leave your post for the day and get Tina settled. I can handle things here."

"Yes, ma'am," Amy replied, and I half expected her to throw in a salute or something. The two older women went into Lita's office and closed the door behind her.

"I wonder what's going on," I asked, shooting a glance at the now-closed door.

"Do you want to know?" Amy asked with a mischievous grin.

"Well, we can't, can we?"

"That door is sealed with magical powers to stop anyone from listening in, but I figured out a spell ages ago that lets me listen in anyway when things get boring. You have to promise not to tell anyone though, ok?"

"Deal," I agreed. Amy grinned.

"Good. *Jupiter, I really do wonder what is said by the leader of the coven of thunder. Hear her words and let me listen.*"

I heard Lita's voice suddenly, although it was like she was right next to us instead of inside the other room.

"Murdered?" she asked.

"Yes," Aria King's somber voice replied, sounding equally close. "He was found strangled outside The Magic Mule, where he'd spent the evening."

"What's The Magic Mule?" I asked Amy.

"The local bar," she replied, shushing me with her hands so we could keep listening.

"That's terribly tragic. I'll let Myrtle know first thing in the morning."

"We need to keep this under wraps as much as possible. We haven't had a murder here in years; I don't want paranormals to panic."

"Especially not with our new arrival," Lita pointed out, and my eyes widened. That was me.

"Exactly. I believe Drake was with her the entire time until he brought her to me, so there's no way she could have done it, but you know the way people here are."

"Right. I'll make sure she's made aware of what's happened, and that she should keep her head down until this is solved."

"Good, thank you, Lita. I'm going to head back to the crime scene now."

"Kill this spell, or it won't end well," Amy whispered, brandishing her wand once more and waving it at the door. Instantly, the voices disappeared, a second before the door opened once more and Aria left, nodding at us as she strode quickly back out.

"Let's get out of here," Amy whispered to me and we followed Aria out into the dark night.

CHAPTER 6

"*D*id I hear right? Was someone *murdered*? Also, where are we going?"

"Yeah, it sounds like it. Myrtle is – was, I guess – married to Philip Vulcan, one of our coven members. He wasn't exactly the greatest wizard ever, and from what I've heard he spent almost every night at The Magic Mule, but I can't say I'd heard he was involved in anything that might get him killed. As to where we're going, I'm taking you home."

"Lita said you have roommates?"

"She did," Amy nodded, and I realized then that Amy had probably listened in to the entire conversation between Lita and I. Of course she would have; I was a new witch who had shown up in the middle of the night. "Ellie works as a cook at Hexpresso Bean, the local coffee shop. Sara is between jobs at the moment.

Her magic is, well, inconsistent. She's very good on the broom, though."

"And you work for Lita?"

"I do, I work as her assistant. It gives me time to study; I'm working on some advanced magical theory courses with the intention of eventually teaching them."

"Cool," I said, impressed. Amy sounded smart.

"Our house is just here," Amy said, motioning towards a cute wooden chalet with green shutters and a large patio that stretched across the entire ground floor. "Come on in."

I did my best to follow Amy quietly into the house, not wanting to wake up my new roommates. I figured that probably wasn't going to make the best impression. Amy led me towards the back of the room and into a bedroom.

An owl flew over and landed on Amy's shoulder, and while I tried not to stare or point it out, I just couldn't help myself.

"Umm... that's an owl... and he's on you," I said, as the grey bird peered at me curiously. I couldn't help but notice his eyes looked a lot like Amy's.

"Oh yes, this is Kevin. He's my familiar."

"Right. Familiar. I made a mental note to ask what a familiar was later; I just didn't think my brain could handle any more information right this second.

"This one's yours," Amy said, motioning into the

bedroom. "The bed is already made. I'll be here when you wake up and we can get you settled in a bit more."

"Thanks," I said gratefully, a wave of exhaustion washing over me. The events of the night had obviously caught up with me. Amy closed the door behind her as she left, and I didn't even bother turning on the light or changing out of my clothes before absolutely collapsing on the bed.

~

I woke up a few hours later to sunlight pouring through a window. It took me a split second to realize where I was, as the events of the previous night came flooding back to me.

Had that all really happened? Surely, it was all a dream. And yet, here I was, in an unfamiliar bedroom, with a turquoise-and-white color scheme – white bedframe and sheets with a turquoise duvet, white walls with turquoise curtains, rug and armoire – wondering if maybe I'd just gone insane. That was definitely a more likely possibility than the idea that I was *actually* a witch, right?

I yawned, and while a part of me really, really wanted to crawl back into bed and go back to sleep in the hopes that this time I'd wake up in my normal single bed back in Seattle, another part of me was now too curious to sleep, and I eventually decided to head out into the main part of the house.

BACK TO SPELL ONE | 39

I wandered into the kitchen, following the delicious smell of baking, where I found a half-dozen cinnamon buns on a plate, along with a hand-written note next to them.

"Hi there, new roomie! Sorry I wasn't here to meet you, but I hope these rolls make up for it. Try to convince Amy to come by Hexpresso Bean later and say hi."

There was a smiley face, and a scribbled name: Ellie.

I smiled. It looked like my new roommates had been told about my middle of the night arrival.

I went through all of the cupboards in the kitchen until I found a plate, and I grabbed one of the cinnamon buns and began to dig in.

The taste was heavenly, with half melted cream cheese icing dripping down the sides of the delicious pastry. There was more than just that though; it was like with every bite my energy levels grew. By the time I had finished the cinnamon bun, I actually felt like I had gotten a full night's sleep. I looked at the rest of the bun suspiciously. There had to be magic involved in making these, right?

Just then, a tall, slim woman with bright red, curly hair, freckles, and huge green eyes made her way into the room.

"Oh, hi! You must be Tina. I'm Sara," the woman said, grabbing a plate from the cupboard and a cinnamon bun of her own.

"It's nice to meet you," I said. "And it's nice of you to let me live here, too."

"Of course! Besides, there aren't nearly enough witches our age in this coven. Most of the coven witches are older, so it's nice to finally have someone else to hang out with."

"Well, I don't know how much fun I'm going to be to hang out with. After all, I only found out a few hours ago that I'm a witch, and I have absolutely no idea how magic works."

Sara shrugged. "That's not a problem. I've been doing magic my whole life and I still mess it up constantly."

"Does that mean it's hard?"

"It depends on the person. I find it hard. I was always much better at physical activity than magical studies. I might not be able to make a potion to save my life, but I can fly a broom better than anybody who lives in Western Woods."

I grinned. "Can you teach me how to fly a broom then? That sounds awesome."

"Of course! In fact, this morning when Amy was doling out assignments to teach you, she figured that broom flying was definitely my domain."

Amy chose that exact second to walk into the room. "Good, you're up. How are you feeling?"

"Honestly, when I first woke up I kind of thought all of this had been a dream. Also, is there some sort of magic in those cinnamon buns? I feel like I've gotten a full night's sleep since I've eaten one."

Amy gave me a sly smile. "It's good that you noticed. Yes, I told Ellie about last night, and she figured that when you woke up you probably wouldn't be feeling at your best. So, she added an energy boosting potion to the recipe."

"She left a note saying that I should stop by Hexpresso Bean and say hi."

"We can do that, of course. We should also get you some new clothes, too."

I looked down at the clothes that I was still wearing from my last shift work, which seemed like it had been weeks ago: a plain black tank top, and a pair of leggings with simple ballet flats. I supposed it was really all I had, now.

"I, uh, don't really have much money. Plus, what's the currency situation like, here? Do you take US Dollars?"

Amy laughed good-naturedly. "No, we have our own currency. Wow, this is definitely going to be fun. As for money, don't worry about it. The coven will take care of everything until you get on your feet and find a job suitable for a witch of your skills."

"I have a feeling there aren't going to be that many jobs for someone with no talent whatsoever," I said with a small smile.

"You'd be surprised," Sara said. "Even I manage to find something from time to time."

"You're always so down on yourself," Amy said to Sara. "You have skills of your own, even if they're not strictly on the academic side of things."

"It's easy for you to say," Sara replied. "Your mother isn't one of the most famous healing witches in the world."

"Healing witches?" I asked.

"They're the equivalent of what you would call a doctor," Amy explained. "Of course, our healing witches use magic to heal people. It's one of the most difficult jobs in the paranormal world, and requires extensive training. Sara's mother has a reputation for being one of the best."

I suddenly felt a little bit sorry for Sara. I imagined it couldn't be easy to have a mother who was so famous for being so good at magic, especially when Sara sounded like she wasn't that good at magic herself.

"Anyway, we should get going. It is getting late in the day," Amy said.

Sara laughed. "It's barely 10 in the morning."

"Yes, well, the early bird gets the worm."

"And the second mouse gets the cheese," Sara replied, sticking her tongue out at Amy. "You don't have to be so perfect all the time."

"It's fine," I said with a smile. "The faster I get used to everything in this place the better."

"Well, I can join you for a few hours. I have a job interview to do broom deliveries for Plants and Potions later on today, but it's not until 2 o'clock."

"Great!" I had to admit, it was really nice to feel like I actually had friends. Besides, I was about to navigate a whole new world of magic. It was good to have someone on my side who knew what they were doing. Two someones was even better.

CHAPTER 7

"So how far away is Hexpresso Bean?" I asked as the three of us left our little cottage.

"Oh, everything in town is within walking distance. Western Woods is quite small by paranormal town standards, and you can essentially walk from one end of town to the other in 20 minutes," Sara replied. "If you want to go further out into the woods, however, then it's a good idea to know how to use a broom. There is enough nature around that even while staying within the town boundaries you could easily spend a day walking around."

"Is hiking a big thing here?" I asked. It sounded like this was a nice place to go on a few day hikes.

"Why walk somewhere when you can fly?" Amy asked. "Besides, a lot of the shifters use the woods for their own thing."

Right. I'd forgotten about the shifters existing. So, hiking in the woods was out, but I was definitely cool with flying around them.

The three of us walked down the cobbled streets for about three minutes until we reached a narrow brick building with a bright red door. Hanging above the door was an old-fashioned sign that looked about 200 years old with a faded, painted cup of coffee and 'Hexpresso Bean' written in cursive above it.

As soon as we pushed the door open, the wafting aroma of roasting coffee beans and fresh baking reached my nostrils. I stopped and inhaled deeply, enjoying the scent. The interior of the coffee shop was surprisingly large, with tables and comfortable-looking couches spread haphazardly about. A large coffee machine at the back of the room squealed as a barista frothed up some milk, and the low murmur of idle conversation filled the air. Despite the fact that it was midmorning on a weekday, Hexpresso Bean was almost full.

"I'll grab us a table," Sara said. Amy nodded, and motioned for me to follow her towards the front counter, where a woman with long blond hair, brilliant blue eyes, and fluttering golden wings behind her hovered, a polite smile on her face.

"Hello, Amy," the woman – she had to be a fairy – said. "And you must be the new witch in town," she continued, looking over at me.

I nodded shyly. "I'm Tina."

"Well, welcome to Western Woods. Why don't the two of you have a seat, and I'll bring out exactly what you need. I'll make sure Ellie comes out as soon as she gets a minute."

"Thank you, Aurora," Amy replied. "That would be perfect."

"And don't you listen to what anyone around here says," Aurora said, leaning towards us carefully. "As far as I'm concerned, you're completely welcome."

"Oh, she doesn't know anything about that yet," Amy said, and Aurora's eyes widened as she floated back.

"Sorry!" she said. "I didn't mean to speak out of turn."

"It's all right," Amy said. "She's going to find out soon anyway, so it may as well be from you."

"What are the two of you talking about?" I asked.

"I'll tell you when we're at the table," Amy said. I smiled at Aurora as Amy took me by the elbow and led me towards a nook Sara had found. Four overstuffed arm chairs surrounded a small round table, and Amy and I sat down, with me looking at my new friend expectantly.

"I didn't want to tell you earlier, but it turns out last night Aria King was right. Philip Vulcan was murdered, and with word spreading that there is a new witch in town, a few people have made it known that they don't think it's a coincidence."

My eyes widened. "People think *I* killed this guy? I didn't even know him."

"We know that," Sara nodded. "But murders are very rare here. We haven't had one in years. I think people are scared, and they're reacting without thinking."

As I looked around the room, I became all too aware of the eyes on me. I sunk deeper into my chair. I *really* didn't want to be the center of attention right now.

"So who was the man that was killed?" I asked.

"He was a part of our coven. Well, he married into our coven. He and Myrtle met while they were both on holiday in a paranormal town in Hawaii. He was originally from Arizona somewhere, and moved here to be with Myrtle back in the 80s. He's been a part of our coven ever since, although his powers are still linked to Io, a volcanic moon, and his powers were very much strengthened around fire." Amy sighed. "He wasn't much of a wizard, and to be totally honest, I'm not sure their marriage was very happy. Philip was always out drinking, and he hopped from job to job. Still, I can't imagine who would have wanted him dead."

"So how do we stop people from thinking I killed him?" I asked.

"Well, we have to wait for Chief Enforcer King to solve the crime and arrest someone else," Amy said.

"What if she doesn't do it?" I asked. "What if she can't find the murderer?"

"We should investigate ourselves," Sara said, leaning forward in her chair, her green eyes sparkling excitedly. "After all, this affects the coven. But more importantly, if we figure out who killed Philip, it means no one would have any reason to be suspicious of Tina anymore."

Amy gave her an askance look. "Do you know how terrible an idea that is?"

Sara shrugged. "It's not as terrible an idea as doing nothing and leaving Tina here to be a pariah in her new town. Lita told us to make her feel welcome, and frankly, I think helping solve a murder that half the town thinks she committed falls under that purview."

Amy opened her mouth to argue, but before she got a chance to reply, a short woman with wavy brown hair tied back in a ponytail that reached halfway down her back made her way over to us, a huge smile on her face.

"You must be Tina! Hi! I'm Ellie," she said, wiping her hands on the cat-print apron she wore and plopping herself down on the last open chair around the table.

"Hi, Ellie," I said with a smile. "Thanks for the cinnamon buns. They were delicious."

"I'm glad you liked them."

"You'll have to teach me how to make that potion you added to them for energy. That would definitely have come in handy when I was doing my high school exams."

"You got it," Ellie said with a grin. "Now, how do you like the magical world so far?"

"It's unbelievable," I said. "Like, seriously. I woke up this morning and half expected all of this to have been a dream. A part of me still doesn't really think this is real."

Ellie laughed. "That sounds about right. I can't imagine finding out *now* that I was a witch."

"Plus, it's harder with Philip being killed," Amy said. "Apparently, a bunch of people think Tina might have done it."

Ellie's eyes widened. "Oh no, I was hoping she wouldn't find out about that."

"Aurora let it slip."

I put my face in my hands. "Great, so it is true. I've been here less than a day and I'm already a pariah."

"I think we need to solve the murder ourselves," Sara said to Ellie. "After all, the sooner the real killer is found, the sooner Tina's name is cleared, and the sooner she can really get a normal life started here."

I almost laughed at the use of the phrase 'normal'. Nothing about this place was in any way normal. The point was emphasized when just then Aurora came by with what looked like three giant freakshakes - the coffee-filled Mason jars had chocolate sauce dripping down the side, more whipped cream than I could fit in my mouth at once, and they were topped with chocolate shavings, sprinkles, gold shavings, and had a cute straw and a drink umbrella sticking out of them. It was like the coffee Chief Enforcer King had brought me earlier, but taken to a whole new level.

"Here are all your coffees, crew," Aurora said with a smile before floating away, her wings beating at a million miles a minute.

"What *is* this?" I asked, my mouth dropping open.

"Oh, this is a standard Hexpresso Bean coffee," Amy explained. "There's coffee in there, and whipped cream, and the sprinkles are magical – basically, whatever you need for that day, you'll get. So, if you're writing an exam and need to be hyper-focused, you'll feel that. If your boyfriend just broke up with you and you feel like you're going to cry, it makes you feel happy for a little while."

"Wow," I said, eyeing the coffee with a combination of curiosity and fear. "What happens when you drink too many of these and get super fat? Can the sprinkles burn calories?"

Sara laughed. "I wish! You're not really supposed to have more than one a day; the effects of the sprinkles last for twenty-four hours."

"Ok," I said, picking up one of the Mason jars from the table and taking a sip through the straw. To my surprise, it wasn't actually overly sweet. There were definitely chocolate tones to the drink, but I could still taste the rich, creamy taste of the espresso shot beneath it. Licking some of the sprinkles, gold leaf and whipped cream off the top of the drink afterwards, I had to admit, it was one of the better things I had ever tasted.

"It's good, right?" Ellie grinned, as if she had read my mind. "I swear, I've put on a good twenty pounds since I started working here. Anyway, I agree with Sara. We need to investigate this murder."

"Sometimes I swear I'm the only person here with any sort of common sense," Amy argued. "Solving murders is Chief Enforcer King's job. Even if we *did* think this was a good idea, we'd have no idea where to even start."

"I do," Ellie said. "A couple of the coven wizards were in here this morning. Eric Grom and Randy Tonner. They were talking about it; it's how those of us working here found out about the murder. Anyway, Aurora said that they were discussing it while they ordered, and they said that last night at The Magic Mule, Philip had been throwing money around like it was nothing. Apparently, he bought an entire round for the bar."

Amy raised an eyebrow. "That's strange. He had always gone from bad job to bad job; I can't think where he would have gotten that kind of money from."

"Exactly," Ellie said triumphantly. "So there's a lead for you to follow. Where did Philip get that money from, and why?"

"Still," Amy argued, "this isn't our fight."

"Oh come on, you're intrigued," Sara said with a smile as she took another sip of her coffee. "This is a problem, and you can't let a problem go without trying to solve it."

Amy opened her mouth to protest, then closed it again. "Fine," she eventually said. "I'm a little bit curious."

"So that's everyone on board," Ellie said. "Well, that is, assuming Tina is ok with it."

"I think so," I said slowly. "I don't want to get in trouble, though."

"Don't worry, we'll be careful," Sara assured me. "Besides, Amy has been sucking up to everyone in town since she was a baby. As long as she's involved, none of us will get into any kind of trouble."

"I do get the impression that she's a bit of a Hermione," I said with a smile.

"Who?" Amy asked.

"Wait, do you guys not have *Harry Potter* here?" I asked, and I was met with three sets of blank stares. "Wow. Ok, well, I think I'm in. I'd rather not have everyone hate me *straight* away."

It wasn't enough that I had just moved to a strange paranormal town where no one had ever heard of *Harry Potter*; now I was investigating a murder, too.

CHAPTER 8

*A*s we left Hexpresso Bean about half an hour later, I couldn't help but notice on the way out that every eye in the place seemed to be following me. Idle curiosity as people found out about the new witch in town? I hoped so, but I had a feeling it was more than that. Were they wondering if they were watching a murderer leave the coffee shop?

I put my head down and rushed out behind my friends, like some sort of scandal-ridden celebrity doing her best to avoid the paparazzi.

I followed Sara and Amy down the street until we reached a cute little cottage, painted white, with huge windows at street level that displayed mannequins dressed up in all sorts of clothing. One of them wore a long, dark cloak, another, with fluttering fairy wings, had on a cute black summer dress with pink polka dots. The third had on blue jeans and a tight, grey T-shirt with a black blazer on top. My mouth dropped open as the mannequins began to pose as the three of us walked past, moving really quite naturally considering they weren't alive. They weren't alive, right?

"Those aren't, um, real, are they?" I asked Amy as we walked past the window, eyeing the mannequins somewhat suspiciously.

Amy laughed. "No, of course not. It's just magic that makes them move. Randy, who owns the shop, was the one who figured out the spell to make them pose for visitors."

That was a relief. As we walked through the front door, an old-fashioned bell rang to indicate our arrival, and a part of me was a little bit taken aback at how low-tech it was.

The entire store was filled with rack after rack of clothing, but instead of being organized by gender or by type of clothing - undergarments, nightwear, that sort of thing - they were organized by paranormal type.

On the wall to my right, a large sign read "Elves". Next to it was another sign, this one reading "Witches". The sign on the left wall indicated that those clothes were all designed for shifters, and a sign hanging in the middle of the room, presumably by magic, made it obvious that the clothes in the center were all for fairies.

"Come on over here," Sara said, leading me towards the right hand wall.

"Don't vampires live here? Where are their clothes?" I just had so many questions.

"Oh, if you take the stairs to the right, that leads to the basement, where all the vampire clothes are kept. That way they can shop in the dark, which is how they prefer it." Sure enough, there was a set of stairs on the right hand side of the shop, leading to a basement level.

"Yes, but a witch like you could never pull off the clothes a vampire would wear," a man's voice said from behind me, and I jumped slightly.

Turning around, I was faced with a jovial-looking man with a round face, and huge glasses that gave him a real bug-eyed look that somehow suited him.

"With your brown hair, and slightly tanned skin, you absolutely must wear something more colorful than the blacks, whites and navy blues the vampires prefer. It would be a crime against the paranormal community for someone with your complexion to dress in such drab colors."

"Tina, this is Randy, the owner of the shop here," Amy said with a smile. "Randy is an absolute genius when it comes to dressing witches."

"And where might you be visiting from?" Randy asked, as he made his way towards one of the racks and began frantically going through the clothes.

"I'm not visiting, at least, not really. I'm new to Western Woods."

"New, you say?" Randy said, pulling out a gorgeous

blue halter top that seemed to shimmer in the light. "Now this, this will go beautifully with your eyes."

"She only found out yesterday she has magical powers," Sara explained. "This is all very new to her."

"Ah, well it has been quite some time since the coven has found a new member," Randy said. "From one coven of Jupiter member to another, let me welcome you to town."

"So you're a witch as well?" I asked.

Randy laughed. "Technically, wizard is the phrase for a man, but I'm not one to be picky when it comes to gender use. You really *are* new to the magical world, aren't you?"

I nodded, just as something came to me. "Wait, you wouldn't happen to be Randy Tonner by any chance, would you?"

"That's me."

"You were one of the men who saw Philip Vulcan at the bar last night, before he was murdered, right?"

The expression on Randy's face fell. "Yes, what an absolute tragedy. Eric – he's my husband - and I were enjoying a drink after work last night when Philip came in. He seemed happy for once, which was nice. I knew that he was having trouble at home, since Myrtle came in the other week with a number of her friends, loudly discussing her marital issues. Most of them revolved around money."

"But we heard that he actually had money last night," Sara said. I couldn't help but notice Amy was glaring at the two of us; she obviously still wasn't completely sold on this idea.

Randy nodded quickly. "Yes, Eric and I both noticed. He was throwing Abracadollars around like it was nothing. At one point he bought a whole round for the bar."

"Do you have any idea where he got the money from?" I asked. This time, Randy shook his head sadly.

"No, I haven't got a clue. It's quite sad. Philip might not have been the best husband - or the best worker, for that matter - but he wasn't a bad guy. He certainly didn't deserve to have his head caved in outside the bar."

"His head was caved in?" Sara asked.

Randy nodded. "Oh yes, it was really quite horrid. One of the vampires was just coming in to start his shift around eleven. He went around the side of the building to come in through the back entrance, and as he did so he passed the broom rack at the side of the building. That was where he found Philip. He ran inside and called out to us to help, and we immediately did. Unfortunately, it was quickly evident that we were too late to help Philip in any way."

"So Philip must have died sometime before eleven," I mused.

"Oh, it couldn't have been very long before then, either. Patricia Trovao had just finished a double shift, and had a quick drink with Eric and I, and she left just after ten-thirty. She lives on the outskirts of town, so she takes her broom everywhere. Hers would have been on the rack, so if Philip had already been killed she would have come across the body."

"That narrows it down to sometime between ten-thirty and eleven o'clock, then," Sara said.

"Great, now we have a whole bunch of information that we're not going to do anything with," Amy said, glaring at the both of us.

"Oh, come on, Amy," Sara said. "The more we find out, the more likely we are to clear Tina's name sooner rather than later."

"How on earth are you a suspect?" Randy asked, turning to me.

"By virtue of being a new arrival on the night of the murder," I said with a shrug. "I had absolutely nothing to do with it, but that doesn't seem to be stopping the rumor mill."

"No, simple things like facts don't seem to be stopping anybody from making up whatever stories they want these days," Randy said, shaking his head sadly.

"Why don't you try on that top?" Amy asked. "Randy's right, it really does suit you. And you need to start dressing more like a real witch."

On that note, all the talk of the murder ended, and Randy quickly got to work digging through the racks to find me a number of clothes that would make me look like I really fit in here in Western Woods.

Two exhausting hours later we finally left the shop, with promises that a magical delivery system would ensure that the bags of new clothes would be magically delivered straight to the living room at home. I had to admit, Randy really did know what he was doing. I was pretty sure there was some magic involved in the clothes that I now owned, since most of them shimmered or shone differently depending on the angle I was at, or the way the sun hit them. It wasn't until I was in the shop that I noticed that Amy and Sara's clothes all really did the same thing as well.

Witches, it seemed, liked to match comfortable, darker pants, with brighter, more adventurous tops. Sure enough, as we left the store, I couldn't help but realize that I finally did look a lot more like Sara and Amy. I was now wearing a pair of Navy blue leggings and that same light blue halter top that Randy had picked out for me first.

It was nice, in this warm weather in Western Woods that seemed to match the warm Seattle weather pretty well.

"Great, now you look like one of us," Sara said. "Now we just need to get you a wand."

CHAPTER 9

"*S*o is this going to be like *Harry Potter*, where an old guy in glasses finds me a wand that chooses me, based on the hair in the middle and what the wand is made of?" I asked as we walked down the street.

Amy gave me a strange look. "I don't know what this *Harry Potter* you speak of is, but no, not at all. A Witch in Time is the all-purpose store for local witches and wizards. If you ever need anything that's specific to our kind – like a new wand, if you lose yours – then this is where you go."

I couldn't help but feel a little bit disappointed. "Oh, so the wands aren't really connected to their owners at all?"

Sara gave me a smile. "No. I wish that were true, then I could just claim I had the wrong wand. Really, though, wands aren't exclusive to their owners. You can choose whichever wand you want; it'll have the same effect as any other when you're casting a spell."

We entered the store, which was lined with shelves from floor-to-ceiling carrying all kinds of strange instruments I'd never seen before. I could have spent hours in here, but Amy and Sara quickly led me towards the back wall, which was lined with a whole selection of wands.

My mouth dropped at all the *choices* that were on sale. Not only were there wands in different lengths – I saw everything from around two inches long to over two feet – but they were also available in dozens of different colors, some had patterns, and some had carvings ranging from the simple – a little twist going along the side of the wand – to the far more complex – like one that I saw with a face carved out of it, and a pear in the middle, not unlike Lita's wand.

"Now you just need to choose which one you want," Amy said.

"What do yours look like?" I asked, curious. Amy pulled out a plain wooden wand, just under a foot long.

"This is mine. I don't go for anything too flashy. After all, the wand is simply a tool. I let my magic show off my skills instead."

I could see Sara behind her trying not to roll her eyes, and I hid a smile. Sara pulled out a beautiful, shiny, deep brown wand with forest-green leaves carved into the side.

"I, on the other hand, feel that you should feel good

about your wand, and find one that you enjoy looking at. Even though the magic itself might not be better, I think if you enjoy being around your wand, your magic will improve."

"And how's that working out for you?" Amy asked. Sara shot her a glare in return.

"We can't all be little Miss Perfect."

I ignored their jabs at each other and made my way towards the wall. There were so many options, I didn't know which one to pick. Should I go with something classic and plain, like Amy's wand? Or should I pick something a little bit more out-there, like the one that appeared to have been dipped into a vat of pink glitter?

As I looked over the crates of wands, however, one of them caught my eye. I made my way towards it and picked up the light piece of wood. It was nine, maybe ten inches long, and didn't have any markings on it. The wood was perfectly smooth, and painted a gorgeous ivory color, but with a few small, gold flecks embedded in the paint that caught the light and gave it a slightly ethereal look.

"Oooh, I like that one," Sara exclaimed, the argument with Amy forgotten as soon as she saw me holding the wand. I flicked the wand around with a smile, trying to imagine myself using magic. I had to admit, I liked this wand too. It felt practically weightless in my hand, and the flashes of glistening gold gave it that superficial magical feel, which I really liked.

"That is a very nice wand," Amy nodded in agreement. "Good choice."

"I think it's the one I want to get," I finally said with a silly grin on my face. Yup, I'd definitely found my wand.

"Great," Amy said. "Let's take it to the front and buy it."

"We should go visit the hospital next," Sara suggested, and Amy narrowed her eyes at her.

"And exactly why would you want to do that?"

Sara shrugged innocently. "I thought maybe Tina would like to meet my mother."

"Of course you do," Amy said, narrowing her eyes. "And the fact that the hospital was the last place where Philip worked has absolutely nothing to do with that."

"Nothing at all, obviously," Sara said, throwing a wink my way. I hid a smile. I had to admit, I was a little bit torn when it came to the plan to investigate the murder ourselves. Obviously, I wanted to clear my name and make sure that everyone knew I hadn't murdered anybody. But at the same time, a part of me felt that it really was the sort of thing law enforcement should do. And Aria King seemed like she would be a good Chief Enforcer.

The three of us weaved our way through the shelves until we reached the front counter. There was no one there; in fact, I only just realized that I hadn't actually seen anybody since we came into the shop. As soon as we stepped in front of the counter, however, a black curtain leading into the back room was pushed aside, and out stepped a middle-aged woman with frizzy, greying hair and glasses that gave her face an even more pinched and birdlike look than she would have had otherwise.

"Yes?" The woman said as she made her way towards the counter. "You would like to buy this wand?"

"Yes, please," I replied with a nod.

"I haven't seen you around here before," the woman said, tilting her head slightly.

"Tina's new in town," Amy piped up. "She's been adopted by our coven, so to speak."

The woman leaned forward, openly inspecting me, and I had to admit I felt incredibly uncomfortable. I resisted the urge to take a step backwards, but it was tough, as the lady was definitely inside my personal space.

"This is the new witch I have heard about?" the woman said.

"Yes, Ariadne. Tina arrived here last night for the first time, and she has no magical experience. That's why she needs a wand," Sara explained.

"Yes, I have heard about the new arrival. I have also heard about Philip's death, and I find the timing of the two events to be quite a coincidence."

"They are a coincidence; Tina was never alone in Western Woods," Amy said. "Now, if you don't mind, I'd like to pay for the wand so we can go on our way."

Ariadne put her chin in her hand as she inspected me further. I shifted where I stood; this was getting more uncomfortable by the minute.

"I'm not certain I want to sell her the wand," Ariadne said. "After all, what if it turns out that Tina is the culprit? There would be questions asked about me. I don't want to be the person selling a wand to a murderer."

"I'll remind you that as Amy told you, Tina is an adopted member of this coven, and as such you're required to sell her a wand if she requests one. I'm sure Lita would be very upset to hear that this is the kind of hospitality that we give to a new coven member," Sara said, leaning against the counter towards Ariadne. My heart warmed at the way my new friends were sticking up for me. Ariadne looked undecided for a minute, and I was sure she was going to try and argue with Sara, but eventually she relented.

"All right, all right. I meant no offense."

"Why don't you show Tina here a little bit of good-will by giving her 20% off the cost of this wand?" Sara said, and Ariadne grumbled something under her breath before replying.

"Fine, fine. But let it be known that if it's discovered that Tina did kill Philip, I was opposed to this the entire time."

As we left the shop, and made our way back into the Street, I felt even more aware of everyone's eyes on me. How many of them believed, like Ariadne, that I could be a murderer? It was one thing to be told that a few people suspected me, it was entirely another to have somebody almost deny me service because they thought I could have killed somebody.

"I think we should go to the hospital," I said. "I want to clear my name."

To my surprise, Amy nodded along with Sara.

"Wait, you agree too?" Sara said to Amy.

"I do. I thought that it was rash, and I thought that we should leave it to the authorities, but it's obvious now that there really is a group of people out there who think Tina could be a murderer. The sooner the real culprit is discovered, the sooner Tina can start to really fit in here. The way Ariadne Thurman treated her just now was abominable, and it should never have happened. I'm sorry, Tina. No one from our coven should be treating you that way, and I will do everything that I can to help make things right."

I could practically feel tears welling up in my eyes at Amy's words. Between Sara sticking up for me and now Amy, I felt like I really, truly belonged here even though it had been less than twenty-four hours.

"You guys are the best," I said, my voice cracking halfway through the sentence, and the three of us coming in for a big group hug.

CHAPTER 10

*F*ifteen minutes later the three of us were standing in front of a large wooden building painted white with a large, red five-pointed star in the middle.

"No red cross?" I asked as we looked up at it.

Amy shook her head. "No, that's for the human world. The red star is meant to indicate that the Healers here are able to perform magic."

It didn't look quite like a normal hospital. For one thing, there was no ambulance bay at the front, and nowhere labeled emergency. We simply walked through the main set of doors at the front, and found ourselves in a waiting room that this time did look like the waiting room in most hospitals. A nurse dressed in scrubs sat behind the counter, and smiled when she saw us.

"Sara," she said warmly. "How are you?"

"I'm good, thanks Sharon," Sara replied. "Do you know where my mom is?"

Sharon nodded. "I believe she is working in emergency today. If you make your way back there, you'll find her."

Something on the wall to the left caught my eye, and I made my way towards a bulletin board covered in posters warning people about various diseases and other ailments.

Vampire Blood Transfusions – Get the Facts!

Magical Moonshine Abuse – Help is Available

Anaspellactic Shock: Everything You Need to Know

"Are these real things?" I asked Amy, motioning to the bulletin board.

"Absolutely," Amy replied solemnly. "In fact, it's good that you bring it up. I need to make a note to teach you about all of these things when we're doing your lessons. After all, anaspellactic shock is something almost every witch experiences at least once in her life."

I shuddered. I didn't know what anaspellactic shock was, but it certainly didn't sound good.

"Come on, this way." Sara motioned for us to follow her before I got a chance to ask any more questions. We made our way through the building, which apart from the brick walls looked like any other hospital. One thing I noticed, however, was that all of the employees had little badges with different shapes and letters on them.

"What are those?" I asked Amy, pointing at the badge of a man who strode past us.

"Those tell everybody the role everyone who works here plays, and also what type of paranormal they are," Amy said. "Anyone with a triangle badge is a witch, anyone with a circular badge is an elf, anyone with a square is a vampire, and anyone with an octagon is a shifter. The fairies don't get badges, since they only perform hospitality tasks here at the hospital, like administrative jobs. The 'H' on a badge signifies that the person is a Healer, or what you would call a doctor in the human world. Someone with an 'A' on their badge is an assistant Healer, or what you would call a nurse. The shifters have sub-lettering to let patients know exactly what type of shifter they are."

"Okay, so someone with a square badge with an 'H' on it would be a vampire doctor?" I asked, and Amy nodded.

"Yes, medicine is one of the very few roles in the paranormal world where the various paranormals all take on the same role. After all, medicine is so personal, a lot of witches, for example, would not want to be looked over by an elf doctor. And on top of that, the biology can be so different depending on the paranormal, that it can be useful for each type of paranormal to be seen by their own kind. Vampires, for example, have very different blood to the rest of us. A vampire Healer can better understand the blood issues that a fellow vampire is experiencing than say, a witch would."

"What do you mean it's rare for the various paranormals to take on the same roles?" I asked.

"Well, it's been determined in the paranormal world that every different type of paranormal has their strengths, and that is where they work. So, the fairies, who are nice to look at and tend to be the friendliest of the paranormals, work in hospitality. After all, they have no magic of their own, other than the ability to make people feel better. So, their skills are best suited to being the front line workers in the paranormal world. Vampires, on the other hand, work best at night. So they take on most of the jobs that have to be performed after dark. Shifters, who tend to be more physically powerful than the rest of the paranormals, take on roles that require more brute strength: law enforcement, security, that sort of thing."

I nodded, finally beginning to understand. Aria, the lion shifter, was the Chief Enforcer, and Drake, the dragon shifter, had been the person guarding the tree that served as a portal between the paranormal world and the human world.

"And what about witches?"

"We take on the jobs that require a witch's or a wizard's magic. So Ellie, for example, does the baking at Hexpresso Bean, because she's able to use magic to add an extra something to the dough that other paranormals wouldn't be able to."

"But, what if say, I wanted to work in hospitality?" I asked, and Amy looked horrified.

"Why on earth would you want to do that? You're a witch."

"I know, but I mean, it's a hypothetical. What if I wanted to?"

"Well, you just wouldn't," Amy replied. "It's just not done." Amy looked at me like I was an alien.

"So, there's no way to do it?"

"Of course not. Hospitality is fairy work, not witch work."

"Oh," I said dumbly, feeling a little bit put out. I hadn't actually realized until now that every paranormal was slotted into doing a specific job. What if there *was* a vampire out there who wanted to be outside in the day doing landscaping? Or a fairy who wanted to become a lawyer? Apparently, there was no way for that to become a reality here in the paranormal world.

"I always thought I would make a good Enforcer," Sara chimed in from in front. "I mean, I'd be hopeless at actually *stopping* anyone with my magic, but I'd be great at catching them. As long as I had my broom, there wouldn't be a criminal around who could get away from me."

"There's no way in the world you could ever be an Enforcer, you're not a shifter," Amy said, crossing her arms. Evidently, she was definitely a stickler for the rules.

"Oh, I know, but that's no reason not to think about

it," Sara said dreamily as she pushed through a set of double doors that led into the emergency room.

The three of us stopped in our tracks. While the corridor we had been walking through was quiet and calm, the emergency room was, well, the complete opposite of that.

A number of assistants with triangle badges - indicating they were all witches – pushed three gurneys through the main hall. Running behind the gurneys were witch Healers, all shouting out orders and spells.

"We need the operating rooms, now," one of the Healers shouted.

"I'm calling this a code black. Any available Healers, regardless of species are needed now," another called out.

"I need five pints of type Jupiter blood, stat," someone else shouted to no one in particular.

The three of us stood in place, shocked as we took in the scene before us. There was blood all over the three stretchers, and what looked like teenagers on them.

"There's my mom, I guess we're not going to be able to talk to her for a while," Sara said quietly. I couldn't see who Sara was pointing to, but seeing as only one of the Healers was tall, with fiery red hair that crowned her head like a halo, I figured that one was the one who had given half her DNA to Sara.

Sure enough, it took nearly an hour before Sara's

mother came over to the three of us as we sat in chairs in the waiting area.

"Sara, Amy, how are you?" the woman asked as she made her way over towards us, wiping her hands off with a towel. She looked over at me politely and smiled. "And who is this?"

"This is Tina," Sara explained. "She just moved to Western Woods after accidentally discovering she's actually a witch. Lita has put us in charge of teaching her to use magic."

"Ah, yes, well I'm sure Amy will be very proficient at that job," Heather said, and I couldn't help but notice Sara's shoulders sink slightly.

"Yes, but I'm sure Sara will be an excellent teacher on the broom," I added.

"Oh, absolutely. There's no one better in the coven on a broomstick, although don't tell Esther I said that," Heather replied with a wink. Sara perked up considerably at those words. "It's just too bad she's so hopeless with a wand. So, how did you come to find you were a paranormal?"

"I accidentally ran into an oak tree that was a portal to get here," I answered.

"Wow, well, this must be quite the change for you," Heather said, eyeing me carefully. "I'd love to interview you about the changes in your life, if you don't mind."

"Mom," Sara complained. "Tina isn't a test subject for you to play with."

"I know, I know," Heather replied. "Do you know what coven you belong to?"

I shook my head. "No. I don't know anything about my biological parents at all. Sorry, but I have to ask: what happened here before, with that emergency? Is everyone ok?"

"Yes," Heather nodded. "They're all going to be fine. A couple of wizards were having a duel at the high school, and it got out of hand. A lion shifter got involved trying to help, and the three of them all ended up with serious injuries, but they're all going to be fine." She shook her head. "Teenagers. Now, about your history-"

"Hey mom, did you know Philip Vulcan well?" Sara interrupted, evidently trying to get her mother off the topic of me.

"Not well, no. But he worked here up until a few weeks ago."

"Did you hear he was found dead this morning?" Amy asked quietly, and Heather nodded sadly.

"Yes, we were told."

"Well, there are people in town who think Tina is one of the main suspects, since she only arrived last night and is new in town."

"That's just ridiculous."

"Exactly. But we wanted to know what you thought about him."

Heather gave us a curious look. "You three aren't trying to investigate this murder yourselves, are you?"

Wow, Heather *was* a very intelligent woman. She had picked up on what we were planning to do straightaway.

"No, of course not," Sara lied. "We were just curious."

"Hmmm," Heather replied, pursing her lips before she replied. "Well, so long as you promise not to go after the murderer yourself and take everything you discover to Aria, I suppose it's all right. Philip worked here as a general magical task worker. He did things like cleaning, fixing broken light bulbs, that sort of thing. It wasn't a high paying job, but it also wasn't the type of job that would have earned him many enemies."

"What about any general relationships that he had?" Sara asked.

Heather shrugged. "I can't say that I know of any. Though he did get along well with some of the witch assistants. You should talk to Tim, or Patricia."

"Patricia Trovao?" I asked, remembering one of the names that Randy had given us.

"Yes, that's her," Heather said, looking a little bit surprised. "Why? Do you know her?"

"She was one of the patrons at the bar outside of which Philip's body was found," Amy explained. "She left before the body was found, however."

"Yeah, but if she was the one who put the body there, she could have just killed him and then left," Sara offered. "Then she could pretend that she hadn't seen the body."

I nodded. "If it's a coincidence, it's definitely a big one. I think we should talk to Patricia and find out what her story from last night is."

"All right, I'll leave the three of you to it. But, be careful. Don't do anything too reckless."

Heather left, and I turned to Sara. "Your mom is surprisingly cool about us investigating a murder," I said.

"It comes with the territory when you're a disappointing daughter," Sara replied with a shrug. "If I had been the intelligent young witch my mom had hoped for I'm sure she'd be a lot more concerned about my safety. She says all the right things about staying out of trouble, but she really doesn't care what I do."

"I don't think you're giving your mother quite enough credit," Amy said.

"It's easy for you to say," Sara replied. "You're the witch my mother wishes she had had instead of me. You're the one who knows all the spells and can make them work, and the one who can make potions in your sleep."

My heart went out to Sara, who evidently wished she was better able to please her mother.

"Anyway, let's go find Patricia and see if we can get her to tell us what happened that night."

$\mathcal{A}$my and Sara continued to discuss Heather as we walked through the emergency ward, with me following behind, trailing slightly as I looked around at all the interesting magical healing equipment. There were no IV bags or syringes here; instead bottles of various herbs surrounded a number of cauldrons, and mortar and pestles. Despite the primitive look, I was fairly certain that magical medicine was a lot more effective than the stuff we had in the human world.

The three teenagers who had gotten into the fight were now lying in different beds in the emergency room, privacy curtains half drawn. An assistant was going from bed to bed, making sure the kids were okay. I moved past them, and in the next bed over, where the privacy curtain had been fully pulled back, lay the most incredible looking man I had ever seen.

He had to be an elf: the ears gave him away immediately. They were pointed at the ends, and if *Lord of the Rings* had taught me anything, it was that the elves were the people of the pointed ears. However, he didn't have the same pretty-boy look as Orlando Bloom. His hair was quite dark, in stark contrast to his pale skin. Instead of long, flowing locks, his hair was cut short, but in a way that gave him a permanent just-got-out-of-bed sort of look. His eyes were blue, almost ice-like. They followed me as I looked in, and I suddenly felt like he was penetrating deep into my soul. I averted my gaze quickly, not wanting to stare, although I had to admit I was curious. I had never seen an elf before, after all.

To my surprise, the elf grinned at me. "Well, if it isn't the new witch in town," he said.

I stopped and stared at him for a second. "How do you know about me?"

"Western Woods isn't that big. A new paranormal in town, now that's big news. Even in the hospital, that sort of information makes its way to me."

I suddenly noticed for the first time that his torso was wrapped in gauze bandage.

"Why are you in here?" I asked.

"Got into a fight with a shifter trying to hunt in the human world," the elf replied casually. "Next time I go to fight a dragon, I'll have to bring my fireproof suit." I wasn't sure if that was a joke or not. Honestly, the idea of the fireproof suit seemed completely reasonable in a magical world.

"Oh," I replied dumbly.

"So, what's your name?"

"Tina. Yours?"

"Kyran. Short for Kyrandir."

"And you're an elf?"

"Wow, you *are* new, aren't you? Yes, I'm an elf."

"And why were you hunting shifters in the human world?"

"Because paranormal law enforcement across borders has been in shambles for years, and many of the bad apples choose to commit crimes in the human world, where they know there will be no consequences."

"So, you're like a vigilante?"

"Something like that."

His casual demeanor was so unlike what I had expected from an elf.

"Are you going to be ok? Dragon fire sounds dangerous."

"I'll be fine. I'm just stuck here for a few days. But you'll see me around, don't worry," he added with a wink, and a blush crawled up my face involuntarily. Great.

"Tina! Get over here," Sara called out to me suddenly from the other end of the room.

"I gotta go," I said to Kyran.

"See you," he said with a grin. As I rushed over to

Sara and Amy, I couldn't help but feel a little bit lighter on my feet than I had before.

"Who was that you were talking to?" Sara asked as we left the emergency room and made our way back down the hall. I didn't know where we were going, but Sara seemed to, so I let her lead the way.

"I met an elf!" I told them. "His name is Kyran."

Amy and Sara shared a look. "Kyrandir?" Amy asked.

"Yeah, that's him. What's wrong?"

"Kyrandir has a reputation in town, and it's not a good one. He's the local bad-boy, basically. He's slept with most of the females in town – regardless of species – and he doesn't really work."

"He said he was fighting a dragon shifter in the human world... isn't that sort of security work normally done by shifters?" I asked.

Amy nodded. "Exactly. No one actually pays him to do anything. He used to have a regular job, hundreds of years ago, apparently. I don't know what happened – I wasn't alive back then, obviously, and the stories get changed throughout the centuries – but he's considered a bad apple now. You should definitely stay away from him."

That was strange. The Kyran I had met didn't seem like such a bad guy.

"He didn't seem that bad to me," I offered, and Amy shook her head.

"You need to be careful in the paranormal world,

Tina. Most magical creatures are inherently good, but just like in the human world, there are some who aren't. And you don't have the magical experience to know who you should stay away from."

"Fine," I said quietly, feeling a little bit sad. I supposed Sara and Amy did know this sort of thing a lot better than I did. Still, I wondered what it was that Kyran had done to get himself fired from his job and made an outcast from society.

"We're here," Sara said as we approached a desk. *Assistant Station – Concoctology* was written above the desk on a plain sign.

"What's concoctology?" I whispered to Amy next to me.

"It's the official name for the study of potions," she replied. "Anyone who has a problem that can be solved by something made in cauldron that isn't bad enough to go to the emergency room comes here."

"Ah," I replied, understanding.

"Hi there, how can I help you?" the assistant behind the counter asked with a friendly smile. Her curly, dark-brown hair framed a face with almond shaped eyes and a cute pair of glasses. She had a kind smile, and looked exactly like what I would want a nurse – or, assistant in this world – to look like.

"You're Patricia, right?" Sara asked.

"Yes, that's me."

"My mom, Doctor Neach, told me we should talk to

you. Randy Tonner said you were at the bar last night, where Philip Vulcan's body was found?"

Patricia looked from side to side, then motioned for us to follow her. She stepped out of the Assistant Station and led us into a small break room a couple of feet away which was currently empty. Sitting on one of the chairs, she motioned for us to join her.

"Why are you asking about Philip?"

If Patricia had been one of his friends, I figured honesty was probably the best policy.

"I'm new to town, I only arrived last night. I've only just discovered I'm a witch, and because of the timing, there are people in town who believe I killed Philip, even though I didn't. I didn't even know him. We're trying to find out what we can to help Chief Enforcer King find the person who really killed him."

Patricia looked at the three of us for a minute, and then nodded.

"Alright, I believe you. Especially if Amy Perkins is with you. You have quite the reputation around town for being an intelligent, hard-working witch."

"Thank you," Amy said, a blush creeping up her neck. Amy was *totally* a Hermione.

"Phil was a good man. He might not have been the smartest, and he certainly had his share of issues, but overall he did his best, and he was always friendly, always kind to everyone. Most people here looked down on him because of the work he did, but he was a genuinely friendly person to those who took the time to pay attention to him."

"You were at the bar with him last night?"

Patricia nodded. "Yes. I was having a drink with Randy and Eric. Philip was there, and he was in a good mood. He bought the whole bar a round. I meant to ask him where he'd gotten the money from. He left sometime around oh, I don't know, maybe ten? I left about half an hour after he did."

"And you had taken your broom to the bar?"

"That's right," Patricia nodded. "I only had one drink, so I figured I was safe to fly home. I grabbed my broom and left."

"And you definitely didn't see anything out of the ordinary by the broom rack?"

"Nothing at all," Patricia replied, shaking her head. "I heard that was where they found Phil."

Sara nodded. "Yes, that's what we've been told as well."

"I can absolutely guarantee you that he wasn't there when I went out," Patricia said. "I do wonder why he left the bar and came back, though. I didn't see a single indication that Phil was around when I'd left, and he had left the bar at least twenty minutes before I did."

"Can you think of anyone who might have wanted to hurt him?" I asked.

Patricia shook her head slowly. "Well, not really. Certainly not to murder him. I know he wasn't getting along very well with Myrtle. She was upset that he had lost his job at the hospital, since he was always hopping from job to job. But nothing that would get him killed."

"Why did he lose his job here?" Amy asked. "Did he get into some sort of trouble?"

"To be honest with you, I don't know. Phil never told me the reason, and I didn't hear anyone mention anything about it."

"Thanks for your help, Patricia," Sara said. "We appreciate it."

"Not a problem. I do hope you help to find Phil's killer. He was a good guy, really. He may not have been perfect, but he also didn't deserve to die."

Patricia left the room, leaving the three of us alone once more.

CHAPTER 12

"What do you think?" Sara asked when Patricia left.

"I think we need to find out why Philip was fired," I replied.

"I agree," Amy said. "It might help us to figure out who might have had a grudge against him."

"We should also speak with Myrtle if we get the chance," Sara said. "Although I'd rather wait a couple of days, since after all, she is now a grieving widow."

"The funeral should be soon," Amy pointed out.

"Ok, so for now, we need to find out why Philip was fired," I said. "Who do we ask about that?"

"Caranthir is in charge of the hospital," Sara said.

"What type of paranormal is he?"

"An elf, obviously," Amy said, giving me a you-should-have-known-that sort of look. "Important administrative tasks are the realm of the elves."

"Right, I forgot about that weird rule about everyone having their place," I replied.

Caranthir's office was on the top floor of the hospital, in one of the far corners. A name plate on the door let us know we were in the right spot.

"Why isn't there a last name on this?" I asked, motioning to the plate.

"Elves only have one name," Amy explained as she knocked on the door. "Caranthir means sun-god in the elvish language. They don't do last names, like the rest of us do."

"Yes?" came a deep voice from inside. We opened the door to find the head of the hospital seated behind a large white desk. In fact, everything in this room was white, from the walls to the bookcase and even the frame which held a certificate of some kind hanging on the wall. The only exception was a large painting of a sunrise, framed against the wall on the right, the only thing in the room that showed any kind of personality, and even it looked relatively cliché.

Caranthir himself was exactly what I imagined when I thought of elves, not like Kyran at all. He had the same pointed ears, but his hair was so light it was practically white, and reached straight down to nearly his waist. His eyes were dark and deep-set; it was almost like looking into space. He wore a loose off-white robe, and if my mother had been here she would have taken one look at his posture and gone "See, Tina?

Just like that gentleman is doing, not slouched over like you always are."

"Sara, Amy, how are you? And you must be the newcomer in town," he greeted us. I gave a small smile. Elves were weird. How did they always seem to know who I was straight away?

"Hi, Caranthir," Sara said. "Can we chat for a second?"

"Of course. What can I do for some of the fine witches of the Coven of Jupiter on this fine afternoon?"

"We were hoping you could tell us why Philip Vulcan was fired from his job here," Sara said.

"Ah. Poor Philip. I heard of his tragic demise this morning. My thoughts are with your coven, of course. I was so saddened to hear that something so horrible would happen to a man so simple. He was not, of course, the most talented wizard to have ever worked in this hospital, nor was he required to be, of course. However, he always did his work well, and I was quite saddened when I came to the realization that I had to let him go."

"But why?" Sara asked again. "What was the reason?"

"That, I'm afraid, I cannot tell you. It would be a severe breach of employee confidentiality."

"I don't think he minds anymore," Amy said, and Caranthir gave her a hard look.

"All the same, Philip still has family in the coven, and they may believe differently. I'm afraid policy is policy, and there is no way that I am able to tell you what it is you want to know."

Wow, this guy definitely did not use one word when ten could do.

"Alright, well, thanks Caranthir," Sara said.

"It was my pleasure, witches. Amy, I should let you know that we have an opening for a Healer coming up in approximately eight months. I am well aware that the training to become a Healer ordinarily takes eighteen, but I am certain a witch of your caliber could complete the training on an advanced schedule, should you be so inclined."

A self-satisfied smile crept up Amy's face along with a small blush at the base of her neck. She was obviously pleased with the compliment.

"Thank you, Caranthir. I will absolutely consider it," she replied before the three of us left.

"So you're going to become a Healer then?" I asked Amy as we left the room and found ourselves back in the hall.

Amy sighed. "No. I would like to. Everyone always assumed I would become a Healer, since it's the most prestigious position a witch in town can have. You have to be immensely intelligent, and skilled in both spells and potions, which many aren't – most witches are good at one, but not the other. But the thing is, I'm actually terrified of blood."

That explained why she looked like she was going to pass out when we had entered the emergency ward.

"Oh. So what are you going to do, then?"

"Well, for now I'm going to continue working for Lita, and I'll continue my studies at the local academy. I'll most likely go into academia, and pass on my knowledge to the future witches," Amy said.

"I think that's a good plan, anyway," Sara said. "You've got so much knowledge that you can pass on, and frankly, I don't want a Healer who might pass out when they see my wounds."

I giggled at the thought of it. "Yeah, that's true."

"Anyway, what are we going to do now?" Sara asked. "After all, Caranthir won't tell us why Philip was fired."

"I suppose we'll simply have to give up on that line of questioning," Amy said. "What else can we do?"

"We could always come back here at night and break in to read the files ourselves," Sara suggested with a sly grin. The look on Amy's face could only be described as one of utmost horror.

"You must be joking!"

"Absolutely not. We need to know what's in those files, and there's no other way to do it."

"I agree," I chimed in. "I mean, as long as we can do it without getting caught."

"Of course we can," Sara said, at the same time as Amy chimed in with, "Of course we can't."

The two girls looked at each other. "It's totally doable," Sara said.

"Right. We'll get caught, we'll be arrested, and not

only will we find ourselves in jail, our reputations will be ruined," Amy said.

"Don't you want to know who killed Philip, and clear Tina's name?" Sara said, wiggling her eyebrows.

Amy sighed. "Don't try to convince me that the law we're breaking is worse than what's being done."

"Is it working, though?"

"Maybe," Amy scowled. "I can't believe you. You're such a terrible influence."

Sara grinned. "You need a little bit of excitement in your life, anyway. When was the last time you went out and had some fun?"

"I don't consider the commitment of a felony to be a fun way to spend a night," Amy replied, crossing her arms. "But if it's what's necessary to find out who killed Philip, I'm willing to do it, I suppose."

"That's all I wanted to hear," Sara replied.

"But for now, we're heading home. After all, Tina has a new wand, and now she needs to learn how to use it."

*a*s soon as the three of us got back home, I marveled at the sight of the clothes we had ordered, sitting in the middle of the living room. Evidently, Randy's magical delivery service had done its job. Amy's familiar, the creepy owl Kevin – who names their owl Kevin, anyway? – sat on top of the cabinets, looking down on us.

"I'm going upstairs to have a nap," Sara announced when we got back. "Who knew that murder investigations could be so exhausting?"

"What about you?" I asked Amy. "You've been up for what, a whole day? Don't you need to sleep?"

"I have a special potion that allows me to stay awake and alert when needed, don't worry about me."

"Yeah, you're definitely a Hermione." That awakeness potion definitely sounded close enough to a time-turner for me.

"Who's Hermione? A friend of yours from the human world?"

"You really haven't heard of *Harry Potter* at all, have you??"

"What's Harry Potter?"

"It's a series of books and movies from the human world, about a teenager with magical powers. Don't tell me you, as a witch, have never heard of it?"

Amy laughed. "No, we don't really pay much attention to the popular culture of the human world. We have our own movie industry, based out of Spellywood, a magical town in California. Our movies are much better; they involve magic."

"Well, one day I'll watch a magical movie, and you can watch *Harry Potter* with me and see just how much of a Hermione you are."

"Alright, that works for me. But for now, I want to get through your first magical lesson."

"Right," I said, pulling out the wand I had bought. I had to admit, it felt pretty cool in my hand. I swished it around here and there, pretending I was actually doing magic, like I was five years old again.

"Ok, hold on a minute," Amy said, returning a moment later with a blank journal and a pen. "You're going to want this to write spells in."

"So all the magic comes with pre-determined spells?"

"Exactly. Unfortunately, the spells are very coven-based. A coven whose powers come from Mercury will have different spells to ours, for example. So, since you're not from our coven, your magic isn't going to work as well when you use our spells. However, it's the only option we've got right now, at least until we figure out exactly where your coven gains its powers from."

"Ok," I said, nodding. Basically, I was going to be a terrible witch until we figured out where I belonged. I was a little bit demoralized about this – who *didn't* want to turn out to be a super powerful witch who somehow had greater powers than everyone who had done this their whole lives – but I convinced myself that frankly, just using magic at all was pretty cool, and the sort of thing that even twenty-four hours ago I could never have imagined.

"So, I thought we should start with the simplest of spells: creating light," Amy said. "While the wand is the conduit through which your magical powers will be displayed, you can always give it help. Focus your energy on the wand as you're saying the words, and the magic will work better. Watch."

Amy flicked off all the lights in the kitchen, and closed the blinds, until we were immersed in almost complete darkness.

"Jupiter, with all your might, I beseech you to fill this room with light."

I gasped as the tip of Amy's wand was suddenly illuminated with a disk of light so powerful I almost had to cover my eyes. A moment later, the light disappeared. Amy went back to the window and drew the curtain back, but only halfway, leaving the room dark, but not pitch black.

"That was insane," I said, and Amy smiled.

"It's one of the easiest spells to learn and to get right," she replied. "Remember, all you need to do is focus on the wand. Do you remember the words?"

I nodded, swallowing hard. It was all good and fine to be told I was a witch, but standing here with a wand about to actually try a spell was a whole different story.

"Great. Let's see it."

I took a deep breath and closed my eyes as I did my best to really focus on my wand. I tried to think of it as an extension of my body, and to feel my life force moving towards it in my right hand.

"Jupiter, with all of your might, I beseech you to fill this room with light."

I gasped as the tip of my wand emitted the tiniest amount of light. It wasn't more than I'd have gotten from a lighter, but it was something!

I had just done magic. This wasn't some sort of elaborate prank after all. I really, truly was a witch.

Wow.

"Good! Now, do it again, but this time, don't use the word 'of'," Amy instructed. "It's 'Jupiter, with all your might', not 'all of your might'."

"Shoot," I mumbled. "Ok, let me try again."

I took a second to re-focus my energy before I tried it again. This time, I focused on saying the words correctly.

"Jupiter, with all your might, I beseech you to fill this room with light."

This time, the light that sprung from my wand could be accurately described as 'similar to an iPhone flashlight'. That was definitely an improvement!

"Awesome," I said, unable to wipe the grin off my face. This was phenomenal. I was doing actual magic. Eleven year old me would be bouncing off the walls with excitement if she had known *this* was going to be in her future.

"Good, you're getting it," Amy said, nodding. "I want you to write that spell down in this book."

"Is it ok if I get a journal from the human world and use that instead?" I asked.

"Of course," Amy replied, nodding. "You can get it when we go back to get your things."

I grinned. I was totally going to go to the local bookstore and buy myself a Gryffindor journal to write my spells in.

"Now, I want you to keep working on that one spell."

"Really? Can't you teach me to do something really cool?"

"Like this?" Amy asked with a grin, flicking her wand towards the kitchen. A second later, the cutlery flew out of the drawer and began dancing on the countertop, sending Kevin screeching away. The poor owl obviously hadn't seen that coming.

"Exactly like that," I laughed. "How did you do that without the words, anyway?"

"The words are a necessary part of each spell," Amy said. "However, as your powers improve, you'll find that it's not always necessary for you to say them aloud. I can simply think the spell, and my wand can hear the words in my head, so to speak. Someone like Sara, however, still needs the words to make the spell work."

"And even that doesn't always work," Sara muttered as she came into the kitchen, grabbing a glass from one of the cupboards and filling it up with water.

"Hey, I'm sure you're better than you think you are," I offered up.

"She is, she simply doesn't have the confidence to do the spells properly, in part because of the constant pressure from her family to be one of the best witches in town," Amy replied, shaking her head. "Sara, you have to stop caring what your family thinks of you."

Sara sighed. "Easy for you to say, you're the smartest witch of our generation. You know Amy got invited to attend Spellford, one of the most exclusive witch colleges in the world?"

"Wow," I said, impressed. "That's pretty cool. Why didn't you go?"

"I, um, thought that I could do better work here, and the academy here is excellent as well," Amy said.

"She's afraid to travel," Sara mouthed at me from behind Amy, so she couldn't see. I nodded. So Amy was afraid of blood, and of traveling. And that was only what I'd discovered in the first twenty-four hours.

"Anyway, that spell is your first assignment. Keep practicing it, and you'll start to get the hang of how to really channel your energy into the wand. The better you are at it, the brighter your light will be. And remember, it's never going to end up being *that* powerful; not until we find your coven, at least."

"Ok," I nodded. "That sounds good."

"Ellie should be back from work any minute. When she gets back she'll teach you how to do potions, and everything that goes with that – learning herbs, that sort of thing. And Sara, did you source out a new broom for Tina?"

Sara burst into a grin as she nodded. "I certainly did! It's one of the best beginner brooms out there. It was actually the one I learned on. I went and grabbed it from my mom's house just now."

"Good," Amy nodded. Evidently, she was taking being in charge of my magical education seriously. "I need to go to work. Will you text me about tonight?"

"Of course," Sara nodded. "I'll take Tina back to the human world to get her things."

Obviously satisfied that everything was going according to plan, Amy got up and began to head out, with Kevin flying after her.

"Have you and Ellie got familiars, too?" I asked, and Sara nodded.

"We do, yes. Mine is a cat named Cupcake who likes

to hide away from the world. You probably won't see her for a few days; it takes her a while to get used to new people being in the house. Ellie has a little Pomeranian, Chestnut, but we all call him Nuts because he's a bit crazy. She sends him to familiar daycare while she's at work, since otherwise he just has too much energy to stay cooped up at home all day, so you'll meet him when she gets back."

"How do you get a familiar? I mean, will I get one?"

Sara nodded. "Of course. In fact, as soon as you entered the paranormal world for the first time, your familiar should have been alerted. He or she will be making their way here, and they're going to try to find you."

"How will I know it's mine?"

"You will be able to hear your familiar's thoughts, and they can hear yours."

"Oh, so as soon as I find a talking owl, I know that's my familiar?"

"Definitely. Though familiars can take the form of any animal. You won't know until you find them. Now, how about a glass of wine while we wait for Ellie before we go and get your things?"

A glass of wine right now sounded amazing.

CHAPTER 14

*A*bout ten minutes later the front door opened, quickly followed by the pitter-patter of little feet running as fast as they could along the hardwood floors, before a giant, blurry ball of dark brown sped past us and back towards the front door.

"There, now you've met Chestnut," Sara laughed. About fifteen seconds later the dog came running back into the kitchen, his little tongue hanging out of his mouth as he panted from the effort of the zoomies around the house. Two black eyes and a black nose poked out from the Pomeranian's furry little body, and as I reached down to pat him he ran over to me, eager for some human loving.

"Hey, guys," Ellie said as she entered the kitchen a moment later. "Has Amy gone to work already?"

"Yeah, it's totally a coincidence that she had to work

before we went to the human world to get Tina's things."

"Right," Ellie laughed.

"So Amy's afraid of traveling?" I asked.

"And everything else under the sun. Spiders, snakes, heights, portals, blood, you name it. If it's a phobia, Amy has it."

"She didn't go to Spellford because she was afraid of the portal to get there?" I asked, amazed. "Does that mean she's never left Western Woods?"

"Exactly," Ellie nodded. "It's a shame. Spellford would be a wonderful experience for her; I've only heard good things about it. And they've actually left the invitation for her open. She could choose at any time to go there after all. But, she won't go through the portals."

"Wow," I said, shaking my head. For someone like Amy, who was totally a Hermione, I could only imagine what kind of fear she must have had to refuse acceptance to the magical world's most prestigious learning institution.

"So, let's get going. I haven't been to the human world in years," Ellie said, clapping her hands excitedly. "We totally need to get those things – what are they called – tacos."

"Do you not have tacos here?" I asked in horror. That was definitely a strike against the paranormal world.

Sara shook her head sadly. "No. Though there are

paranormal worlds a bit further south that do them, sadly, no one here does them."

Well, at least the human world was only a portal away if I ever really needed a fix. "Alright. Well, we'll stop by my apartment, I have to buy a journal, and then we'll get tacos and come back here."

Ten minutes later, after Ellie changed out of her work clothes, the three of us headed out to get my things from my apartment.

"Are we going to go through the forest and see Drake?" I asked.

Ellie nodded. "Yes, that's the easiest portal to use to get to your apartment."

"It's the middle of the day though, won't there be people noticing if three people all of a sudden appear out from inside a tree?"

"The tree is enchanted; basically, anyone who notices us appearing from it immediately has their memory altered, so they think that we were there the whole time."

"Kind of like platform 9 ¾," I muttered to myself.

"Like what?" Sara asked.

"Nothing," I replied, making a mental note to grab a copy of all of the *Harry Potter* books while we were at the bookshop. After all, my constant references were totally lost on my magical friends right now.

Walking through the forest during the day was far less creepy than it had been the night before. The walk also felt as though it was far faster, and pretty soon we reached the clearing, with Drake guarding the portal.

"Good afternoon to the newest member of the coven," Drake said as the three of us approached. "And how are you witches doing on this fine afternoon?"

"Great, thanks. We are taking Tina back to the human world to get her things; we should be back in a couple of hours."

"Sounds good, I'll be here."

Oddly enough, once I actually knew what the portal did, I was a little bit apprehensive about stepping back into it. I could suddenly understand a little bit where Amy was coming from. On the other hand, I had gone through the portal before, and nothing had happened.

Luckily for me, I didn't even have to go first. Sara confidently strode straight up to the tree and walked right into the trunk, disappearing immediately.

"After you," Ellie said, motioning towards Eddie the tree.

I took a deep breath, and tried not to look nervous as I walked straight towards Eddie, every instinct in my body telling me to stop before I walked right into the tree. At the last second I closed my eyes instinctively, and when I opened them two steps later, my nose not hurting from impact, I was back in downtown Seattle. Sara was standing just a couple of feet away, grinning like a crazy person as she looked around.

"I haven't been here in so long; I forgot how quaint the human world looks."

I laughed as Ellie popped out of the tree next to me. "I can't believe this place is actually weird to you guys."

"Absolutely. Why spend any time in the human world when the magical world has so much more to offer?"

"Why didn't you tell us the guy guarding that portal was so hot?" Ellie interrupted.

"Drake? The dragon shifter?"

"Yeah, he's amazing," Ellie swooned. "I'm going to have to find a reason to come here more often."

Our first stop was my apartment, where I hurriedly packed a few things in a duffel bag, trying to push back the thoughts of how sad my life was that I could easily fit everything I needed into a seven gallon bag. After all, this wasn't my life anymore. My life was now in Western Woods.

The Barnes & Noble at Pacific Place wasn't too far from my apartment, and that was where the three of us made our way next. I bought not only *Harry Potter*, but a decent handful of old favorites and new books to read as well. After all, I wasn't sure when I was next going to come to Seattle, and I didn't know what the book situation was like in Western Woods, but seeing as no one had gotten any of my references yet, I had a sneaking suspicion that these were the last human books I'd be able to read for a while.

Besides, my duffel bag was barely half full. Why not take all the books that I could over? It wasn't like I was going to be needing US dollars anytime soon. I had no idea what the exchange rate with Abracadollars was, anyway.

"Ooh, this looks interesting," Ellie said, looking over the copy of *Murder on the Orient Express* that I had picked up.

"You're welcome to borrow it, of course," I said. Before checking out, I made my way to the journal section, where I very happily found a set of *Harry Potter*-themed journals, and I picked up three copies of a large notebook with the Gryffindor logo on the front. After all, my plan was to learn as many spells as possible, and I imagined there existed enough of them to fill more than one notebook.

By the time we left Barnes & Noble, my duffel bag was definitely on the heavier side. When we reached my favorite taco truck and ordered, eating our tacos on the bench nearby, I was happy for the rest.

"Have you given any thought to your eventual career path yet?" Ellie asked. "I know there's no rush, Lita will make sure that you're taken care of while you learn magic, but I'm curious as to whether or not you have an idea."

I shook my head. "No, I don't have a clue. To be honest, I'm just starting to wrap my head around the idea that magic exists, and also that there are only specific jobs that witches can do."

Ellie nodded. "I can understand that. I was lucky; I've always loved baking and everything to do with the kitchen, and there are so many magical baked goods out there that only a witch can make."

"And I have the opposite problem," Sara moaned. "There are no jobs out there for witches whose only talent is riding a broom."

"I'm sure you'll find something," Ellie said sympathetically. "You just haven't found your niche yet."

"It would be nice if my niche could get over here soon, it would stop my mom from constantly remarking on my magical abilities. Now, it's getting dark, and I hate walking through the forest at night. Let's go back to Eddie."

A quarter of an hour later the three of us were back in the paranormal world. It was funny, looking around to Seattle one last time before I left for goodness knew how long. Even though I had lived there my entire life, ever since my parents had died it had no longer felt like home. And now, knowing that Western Woods existed, it felt even less so. While a part of me had expected to feel a little pang of longing as I looked over the city that was all I knew, I didn't feel that at all. In fact, all I felt was a desire to cross back over into Western Woods, and truly start my life and my new home.

"How was your trip, witches?" Drake asked as we made our way back through the portal.

"Great," I said, holding up the duffel bag. "I'm all set for life here in Western Woods."

"I'm glad to hear it," Drake said. "Unfortunately, I'm not able to offer you an escort back into town today."

"Are you sure?" Ellie said, fluttering her eyelashes slightly at Drake. "It's just so scary in the woods at night."

I had to smile at Ellie's shameless flirting. Drake looked a little bit disappointed as he answered. "I'm sorry, rules are rules. I'm not allowed to leave my post, except in emergencies."

I half expected Ellie to pretend she was having a heart attack or something, just so that she could get Drake to take her back to town, but she just pouted slightly.

"All right, well, hopefully I'll have a reason to visit the human world again soon," Ellie crooned. Sara practically dragged her by the arm towards the forest.

"You're ridiculous," Sara said.

"Well, how was he going to know I was flirting with him if I don't make it obvious?" Ellie replied. "Besides, he spends his whole day guarding the portal that I bet like one person a day uses. He might be lonely."

"And if he isn't, I bet he doesn't want some witch throwing herself all over him," Sara replied.

"I'll never know if I don't try."

I hung behind the two of them slightly, simply enjoying the view of the forest as we meandered along the path. Night was definitely falling now, and the first of the Hotaru began lighting the path for us. It was just as magical as the previous night.

As we approached the town center, a sudden commotion started in one of the alleys. The three of us stopped, looking around to see what was going on. Ellie and Sara instinctively pulled out their wands, and as soon as I noticed they were holding theirs I did the same, despite the fact that I only knew one spell, and I didn't even know how to do that one very well.

Still, at least I *looked* like a witch, right?

A black blur came running out from the alley, followed by four boys who looked to be about twelve, maybe thirteen years old.

"Get it!" One of the boys yelled. "He's getting away!"

As the black blur came closer, it became obvious that it was a cat. A cat with something in his mouth.

"What is that?" I asked, squinting at the cat, trying to figure out what it had taken that the boys so desperately wanted.

"It's a gold watch, obviously," the cat replied, and I gasped at the reply. The cat was talking to me! For a second, I thought I was going insane, until I remembered what the girls had told me about familiars.

"Are you my familiar?" I asked. After all, the only cat whose thoughts I should be able to understand were my familiar's.

"Not for very much longer if these boys have their way," the cat replied, running towards me. "Although, no offense, but you don't look like you're that good of a witch."

"None taken, because quite frankly, that's accurate."

The boys were now only about 30 feet away.

"Does that mean I should try and make a run for it?"

I looked over at the other two witches. "Ellie, Sara, this cat is my familiar and we need to protect it," I told them.

The two of them nodded in understanding and stepped forward, protecting me and the cat, who jumped up onto my shoulder.

"Hey, boys," Sara said. "What's going on here?"

At the sight of two fully grown witches, the boys stopped suddenly, all four of them breathing hard.

"That cat's got my watch," one of the boys answered, pointing to the black cat. Sure enough, there was a gold watch in his mouth, and I had a sneaking suspicion that this cat hadn't bought it at the store.

Ellie looked at the watch carefully. "That's funny, that looks a lot like Handromir's watch."

"Well, it's not anymore," one of the other boys said defiantly.

"So if we go and find Handromir and ask him where his watch is, he'll tell us that it's yours, fair and square? There won't be any mention of theft?" Sara said, folding her arms over her chest.

The boys shifted their feet, looking between one another guiltily.

"That's what I thought," Sara said. "Get a move on, and we'll make sure Handromir gets his watch back. And if I see you boys stealing again, I will report you to Chief Enforcer King."

Evidently deciding to cut their losses, all four boys

glanced at each other for a second before running back off into the night.

"I could have taken them," the black cat said, dropping the watch into my hand. I gave him a sharp look.

"Is that right?"

"Absolutely. I'm an expert in martial arts. I know Katrate, and Tae Cat Do."

"I don't think those are real martial arts."

Sara and Ellie had confused smiles on their faces. I could only imagine how crazy this conversation must have sounded to someone who could only understand my half.

"Well, the important thing is we have the watch now."

"Only temporarily; this watch is absolutely going back to its rightful owner."

"Great. Of course I would get a human with morals."

"Right. Well, don't worry, I don't have that many rules, but no stealing is definitely one of them."

"Spoil sport," the cat muttered.

"So I think it's safe to say your familiar has found you?" Sara asked, and I nodded.

"Yes. His name is - wait, what is your name?"

"As I am a martial arts expert, my name is Mr. Meowgi."

It took all the effort I could muster not to burst out laughing at that. Though I had to admit, it was strangely fitting.

"All right, Mr. Meowgi, welcome to the family," I said, motioning to Ellie and Sara. My new familiar did something that I was pretty sure was supposed to be a bow at my two roommates, who both leaned over and began patting him on the head. Letting out a contented meow, Mr. Meowgi enjoyed the attention for a minute until we began heading back home.

"If you give me that watch, Handromir comes by the coffee shop every morning. I can give it to him tomorrow, and tell him that we rescued it from the shifter boys."

"Who is Handromir?"

"He's one of the elves in town; he works as the town's lawyer to defend any paranormals who have been accused of a crime."

"So, like a public defender," I said.

"Sure," Sara replied. "I don't know what that is, but it sounds about right."

"I still think you should let me keep the watch," Mr. Meowgi muttered.

"Absolutely not," I replied. So my new familiar was obsessed with martial arts, and had a bit of a kleptomaniac streak to him. But hey, no one's animals were perfect, right?

CHAPTER 15

*A*s soon as we got back home, Mr. Meowgi jumped off my shoulder and began investigating the house. About five seconds later, however, Chestnut came flying in from the living room, and my new familiar let out a high-pitched squeal as he ran up the side of the nearby couch.

"Don't worry," Ellie called out to Mr. Meowgi. "He's actually really good with cats."

"*Now* you tell me," my familiar replied. "Besides, just because he is good with cats doesn't mean I'm good with dogs."

I had to admit, he had a bit of a point there.

"Well, you'd better learn, because Chestnut has been a resident here for longer than I have," I muttered. Chestnut stood at the bottom of the couch, looking up at Mr. Meowgi, his tail wagging furiously.

"I'm far too good for dogs," Mr. Meowgi replied,

delicately walking across the back of the couch and making an elegant leap onto the bookcase on the other side. Evidently, his plan to avoid Chestnut was going to involve staying higher up than the dog could reach. So long as they weren't actively fighting, I knew they'd eventually get along.

"There's also an owl here, somewhere. Don't try and fight the owl," I warned Mr. Meowgi. "And another cat, but he's shy."

"Thank goodness the cats outnumber the other animals, at least," Mr. Meowgi said.

"I'll let you get settled. Our bedroom is the third down on the left," I called out as I took my duffle bag which was frankly more full of books than anything else, down to the bedroom and dropped it off.

When I got back to the kitchen, the girls had opened a bottle of wine and poured a glass for me.

"You're going to want some of this," Ellie said. "After all, I texted Amy and she's going to take her break in an hour. That's when we're going to go back to the hospital and find out why Philip Vulcan was fired."

"I'm not sure committing a felony when I've been in town less than twenty-four hours is a good idea, but I also don't want to spend the rest of my life living like a pariah here, so I'm in," I said, taking a swig of the wine.

"Am I coming too?" Mr. Meowgi asked.

"Not a chance," I answered. "Too dangerous."

"Danger is my middle name."

"In that case, I'll have to change your name to Austin Meowers."

"Ew, that's an awful name. And I don't understand the reference."

"And yet you understood Mr. Meowgi?"

"In my training I spent time in the human world, and have seen many of their martial arts movies. But the name was given to me by an elf who has spent a lot of time in the human world."

"Ah," I replied, nodding. "Well, one day I'll find us a copy of *The Karate Kid* on DVD. Do you guys have DVDs here?"

Sara and Ellie looked at me blankly, and I sighed. "Ok. Well, one day I'll figure it out."

Forty minutes later, the three of us were getting ready to head out. "Put on some comfortable shoes," Sara said. "After all, we're going to be invisible, but we don't want to be heard, and we want to be able to run away easily if it comes to that."

"Luckily, I only have one option, and they're pretty comfortable," I said, slipping on my flats. After all, I had been coming home from work, and spending eight hours on my feet would have been nigh-on-torturous if my shoes hadn't been insanely comfortable.

"Great. We're going to take the brooms to get to the hospital. Not only will it be faster, but it will minimize the chance of us running into anyone. Alright, ladies. Phones on silent."

I had a sneaking suspicion this wasn't the first time

Ellie had broken into somewhere. I glanced at my phone. Unsurprisingly, it said 'No Service'.

"I'm going to have to get a phone plan here," I muttered, almost to myself.

"We'll take care of that for you tomorrow," Sara said. "Now, since you don't know how to ride a broom, I'll get you to ride with me."

The three of us left the house, with Mr. Meowgi still grumbling about how if we needed a martial arts expert we were going to regret not taking him. I followed the other two to the side, where three broomsticks leaned casually against the side wall of the house. One of them was significantly shorter than the others, and thinner as well. I figured that was the one I was eventually going to be learning on.

Sara and Ellie each grabbed a broom. "We'll do the invisibility spell before we go, but first I want to teach you how to get on," Sara said. "You just hoist a leg over the top, then hold on to me. Cross your legs underneath you for support, and don't think about sliding off. The broom will balance you."

"Ok," I nodded.

"You're not afraid of heights, are you?"

"No, but I've also never ridden a two-inch wide piece of wood high into the air before, either."

"Well, don't worry, I'll try and stay pretty low for now," Sara said. "Now, time for the invisibility spell. This one Ellie is going to take care of."

Ellie pulled out her wand – I wasn't entirely

surprised to find it was long, bright purple, and covered in glitter – and pointed it towards me, first.

"Jupiter with your power so mythical, turn this woman in front of me invisible."

I gasped as all of a sudden I disappeared. I touched my face, and luckily, I felt something there, but for the life of me I could no longer see any part of me. I mean, I knew that was what an invisibility spell did, obviously, but knowing it in theory and actually seeing it in real life were two very different things.

By the time I'd gotten over the shock – and the coolness – of it, Ellie had repeated the spell on Sara, and the broom she held was now hanging in mid-air.

"Tina, if you get lost or separated from us, meet back at the house," Ellie said. "We'll reverse the spell here. Do you know how to get back here on your own?"

I nodded, then realized there was no way Ellie could see it. "Yeah, I think so."

"Good. We're meeting Amy on the roof of the hospital. Now, get on the broom, and I'll make that invisible as well."

Sara's broom shifted as she climbed up onto it, and I reached over and grabbed it, hoisting my leg over and grabbing at my friend's invisible body. I had to admit, I probably would have been a lot more comfortable learning to ride a broom if I could actually see it, and myself.

Still, I knew there were no other options. A second

later, Ellie repeated the spell, and the broom underneath me disappeared.

"Ready?" Sara asked. I squeezed her waist more tightly as I answered in the affirmative.

A moment later the broom began to rise up into the air, and I gasped as my feet left the ground. I crossed my ankles, the way Sara had suggested, and held onto her tightly, simply trying not to move too much. After all, not only did I not want to fall off the broom, but I also didn't want to make it more difficult for her to fly.

It didn't take long before I realized that the others had been right about Sara being skilled on the broom. She kept it flying low, only about 15 feet in the air, but it was high enough that we soared above the heads of all the residents in town. The ride was smooth, and while I initially closed my eyes, it didn't take long before I opened them and took in the view along with the cool night air that whipped in my face.

The view in town at night was quite frankly stunning. The wrought-iron lamps cast a warm glow on the streets of town, and if there had been snow I would have easily believed that this could be some sort of Swiss Alpine village. Well, except for the total lack of mountains. The dark forest in the back gave the warm glow of the town an even more ethereal feel, and I made a mental note to come up here and just look over the town when I eventually learned to ride a broom. I had never seen anything quite like this place before.

CHAPTER 16

*A*s we approached the hospital a few minutes later, I began to relax. I had just survived my first broom trip.

"How are you doing back there?" Sara asked.

"Great, thanks!"

"Just wait until I teach you to ride one of these babies on your own. Riding a broom is awesome."

We landed on the roof of the hospital a couple of minutes later.

"Amy? Are you here yet?" Sara asked.

The silence in the air told us that we were the first to arrive.

"We'll wait for Ellie to get here before reversing the spell. Trust me, you really would rather she do it than me," Sara said with a giggle.

"Well, I know everyone says that you're not the best

at spells, but I have to say that was one smooth broom ride over."

I could practically feel Sara grinning over at me. "It was always the one thing I was good at when we were at the Academy. I love being on a broom. It feels so natural to me, in a way that the spells don't. When I'm on a broom, I feel like I could do anything."

"I love that you have that passion for it," I replied. "I don't really have that with anything. Although, I suppose there's a chance I'll find something in the magical world that I love as much as you love broom riding."

"I assume I'm not the first one here?" I heard Ellie's voice say a moment later.

"Over here," Sara's voice replied a moment later.

"Oh Jupiter, she cannot be seen, although she is here, make this woman reappear."

A second later Sara appeared, as though out of nowhere.

"Where are you, Tina?"

"Right here," I said, with Ellie repeating the spell. As soon as the last of the words left her mouth, my whole body became visible once more.

"Now that's a cool spell," I said, as Ellie repeated it a third time on herself. She cast a slightly different version to make our brooms reappear as well.

"It is pretty handy," Ellie said with a grin. "It's not particularly difficult, but the witches don't teach it until you turn sixteen. I guess they think that kids using it would get into too much trouble."

"I think they have a point," I said with a smile. I could only imagine the kind of trouble I would have gotten into as a kid if I had been able to turn myself invisible at will.

"Well, I was able to do this spell by the time I was eight, and I never got into any trouble," Amy's voice said out of nowhere. Apparently, she had gotten here as well.

"Yeah, but you don't count because of that whole child prodigy thing," Ellie replied as Amy reappeared without speaking a word. "All the cool spells were wasted on you; you were far too much of a goodie-two-shoes to really take advantage of being able to do the spells earlier than the rest of us."

"Perhaps that is why the instructors trusted me with that kind of knowledge earlier than you," Amy said as we made our way towards the roof entrance of the hospital.

I tried the door, but unsurprisingly, it was locked.

"This is an excellent opportunity to train functional magic, instead of simply theoretical, Amy said. "Let me teach you the spell."

"Are you insane? We are absolutely not holding a lesson in the middle of committing a felony," Sara replied. "Just open the door."

"Fine," Amy said.

"Are you sure we should be visible?" I asked. "What about security cameras, or that sort of thing?"

"This is the paranormal world. We don't really need security cameras. Generally, wards and other security spells do the trick," Ellie explained. "This is where Amy comes in handy."

I watched as Amy pointed her wand towards the door. She began muttering a rhyme under her breath, and I didn't quite catch the words, except for 'Jupiter', 'ward', and 'show'. A second later, the door glowed green.

"It's a simple ward," Amy announced happily. "I don't know who the hospital hired to do their security, but this is child's play to get past."

"Great," Sara smiled. "Now get us past it."

It took Amy less than a minute to cast a spell to break the ward, and a second later the three of us slipped into the hospital.

"Caranthir's office is on this top floor, right?" I asked. "That means we shouldn't really run into anybody."

"Exactly," Sara nodded. "All of the administrative staff will have gone home for the night."

The door to the top floor opened up into the office of the administrative section, and the three of us hurried down toward Caranthir's office.

"Time to do your magic again," Ellie whispered to Amy, looking furtively down the hall as though someone might appear any second.

Amy repeated the same spell as before, and once again the door glowed green. After repeating the second spell once more, Amy opened the door, and the three of us were in.

Closing the door quietly behind us, I noticed the room was almost pitch black. The only light came from the light of the moon passing through the window. Ellie immediately strode over there, pulling closed the blinds.

"This time, you know the spell," Amy said to me. I pulled out my wand, and gulped. This was actually a lot more nerve-racking than doing it in the kitchen, when there was absolutely no consequence whatsoever. Here there was a real-life need for the light.

I took a deep breath to center myself as I imagined my energy passing through to my wand, which I had pulled out of my pants pocket. I really had to find a better spot for it.

"Jupiter, with all your might, I beseech you to fill this room with light."

To my surprise, this time, my wand lit up with more light than it ever had before. It certainly wasn't blinding the way Amy's had been, but I was certainly approaching the same amount of light as a small table lamp would have given off.

My three friends began clapping quietly, grins on all their faces.

"You're definitely getting the hang of this pretty quickly," Ellie said.

"Absolutely, it's awesome to see," Sara added.

Amy nodded in satisfaction, then told me that I had to continue holding onto the wand or the connection would break and the spell would end.

I made my way towards a cabinet against the far wall, while Sara sat down at Caranthir's desk, Amy made her way towards a matching cabinet against the other wall, and Ellie joined me.

I pulled out a stack of papers, careful to keep them all in order, as I didn't know much about elves, but I had the distinct impression that Caranthir at least was extremely organized, and would probably notice if it turned out all of his papers were out of order when he showed up at work the next day.

"Has anyone found personnel files of any sort?" Amy asked a couple of minutes later.

I shook my head. "I only have invoices here. And oh boy does this hospital spend a lot of money. Paramedical Inc, Heliosupplies Ltd, Magical Medical Imagery, Western Paranormal Laboratories... there are a ton of suppliers here."

"Yeah, that's the medical business for you," Amy muttered.

"I have the files here," Sara said, pulling out a stack of papers. "I haven't found Philip's though."

The rest of us put what we had been working on away, and made our way to Sara, who split up her sheets of paper four ways.

I thumbed through all of the sheets, looking at

names I didn't recognize, when suddenly Ellie let out a small cry of triumph.

"Got it!"

The three of us huddled around her, with me placing my wand just above the sheet of paper to shed the most light on it. Most of the information was simply clerical: hiring date, firing date, general duties, that sort of thing. It was noted that Philip had never been considered for a raise. However, at the very bottom of the form was a section about the end of employment. In the section beneath, a reason for termination was listed: fired for theft.

The four of us looked at each other. "Was that where he got the money from?" I asked. "After all, he was seen at the bar that night buying rounds and spending up."

"Yeah, but that was a few days after he was fired. I would have expected someone like Philip to have virtually no impulse control. If he had stolen the money, he would have spent it that night, not after being fired," Amy replied.

"That's a good point," Sara nodded. "I wish this had more details. No wonder Caranthir didn't want to tell us why Philip was let go. It doesn't reflect well on the hospital when one of the employees is stealing."

"Well, at least now we have our answer," Ellie said. "Now we just need to figure out what Philip stole. I'd be willing to bet that if it was something important, it could have gotten him killed."

"Drugs, maybe?" Sara offered, and Amy nodded.

"That seems most likely."

Suddenly, I heard footsteps coming down the hall. "Shh!" I said, and the four of us froze. My eyes widened as I realized they were coming towards here.

"Hide," Sara hissed, and the four of us scattered. Ellie and I immediately hid behind the desk, while Amy threw herself behind the floor-to-ceiling curtains and Sara crouched her small frame behind a couch leaning against the side wall.

At the last second, I remembered to drop my wand, immediately breaking the spell and sending the room into complete darkness. Moments later, the footsteps stopped in front of the door, and it creaked open. A second later, the light flashed on overhead. I didn't dare glance to see who it was. It didn't matter. We were caught. Somehow, someone had found us, and now we were all in huge trouble.

I didn't even dare breathe as the person came into the room. When the small trash can next to me was picked up, I almost let out a squeal of fear.

"God I love elves," the person muttered to themselves. "I wish the shifters made as little mess as the elves do."

It was the janitor! This wasn't a security guard. It was a guy emptying the trash.

As every second passed I was sure he was going to notice at least one of us. When the man put the trash can back in its spot, he placed it less than six inches from my foot. And yet, a few seconds later, he left the room, turning off the light and closing the door behind him.

None of us moved for at least two minutes.

"Sweet Jupiter," Sara sighed eventually. "That was close."

"Let's get out of here," Amy said, immediately lighting her wand. Her face was as white as a ghost; I imagined this must have been the closest she had ever come to getting into trouble in her whole life.

"Should we do the invisibility spell first, before we get out of here?" Ellie suggested, and we all nodded in agreement.

"Absolutely."

Sara took me by the hand. "Don't let go, that way we won't get separated when we get back to the brooms."

The next few minutes flew by – and then I was flying, much more literally – back through the air and back home. As soon as we were all safely back in the house, having been magically re-appeared thanks to Amy, who arrived a few minutes after Sara and I, we opened another bottle of wine.

"To freedom, and not being arrested," Ellie toasted, and the four of us laughed in a mixture of relief and insanity.

"See? I told you I would have come in handy," Mr. Meowgi sulked.

"At least it wasn't a waste of a trip," Sara said. "We found out that Philip Vulcan was fired for stealing."

"Yeah, but stealing what?" I asked. "We know Caranthir knows, that was his name on the bottom of the form, but he won't tell us."

"We should find out from Patricia," Ellie suggested, pulling out her phone. "I wonder if she's at the bar right now. After all, it's only just after ten. Let me text a friend I know who works there."

It looked like our night of adventure wasn't quite over just yet.

CHAPTER 17

"Why can't I come *this* time?" Mr. Meowgi whined as I changed into some of the witch clothes I'd bought that morning to go to the bar.

"Because you're not twenty-one, for one thing."

"I am if you count up the ages of all my previous lives."

I didn't know if Mr. Meowgi was joking or not, and to be honest, I was kind of on magical information overload right now, so a part of me didn't even want to know.

"Plus, even in the magical world there have got to be health and safety regulations. I'm pretty sure that even here I'm not allowed to bring a cat into a bar."

"Please, I'm cleaner than most witches," my familiar replied, reaching up and licking a paw as though proving a point.

"Tell it to the health regulation people, not me," I said, giving him a quick pat on the head as I leaned down to slip my shoes on. I was actually starting to enjoy Mr. Meowgi's snarky company. He was a good cat.

The Magic Mule was only about four blocks away from the house, and so the four of us decided to walk there. I was definitely pleased with this new development; one ride on a broomstick was enough for one night, although a part of me was looking forward to future lessons with Sara.

The pub was deep-set in an old, dark building. A rickety old sign above the door announced the bar, and to get to it, we had to pass through an old wrought-iron gate and past a garden patio that honestly looked like it would be amazing to drink at when it was daylight out. With cute little tables and pillow-covered chairs, this was definitely going to be my new ground zero for patio season.

The four of us walked in, and as my eyes adjusted to the light, I looked around. This was basically exactly what I would have expected a small-town pub in England to look like. A large, dark mahogany bar took up the entire far wall, with a cute little fairy who looked to be around twenty fluttering from end to end with a rag, cleaning up. Plush, dark green carpet specked with gold dots lined the floor, and the rest of the floor space was devoted to round tables surrounded by balloon-backed chairs. Large, comfortable-looking booths lined each of the other walls, and Edison bulbs hung from the ceiling, casting a warm glow on everything.

Randy and a tall, heavyset man who I assumed was Eric sat at a table, each one of them nursing a beer. They were obviously in deep conversation. There were about half a dozen other patrons in the bar, none of whom I recognized, but who all looked like witches and wizards.

"Do non-witches and wizards just not drink?" I asked.

"They do, but not at a witches bar," Ellie explained. "This is where all the witches and wizards drink, the vampires all hang out at The Bloody Mary, that sort of thing."

"This place really is segregated, isn't it?" I asked. "Why can't everyone just drink at the same place?"

Amy's look of horror told me that this was something she had never considered. "That just... doesn't happen here," she replied. "Everyone prefers to mingle with their own kind."

I shrugged. Personally, I would have no problems sharing a bar with vampires, or shifters, or fairies, or whoever. But, apparently I was in the minority. As I glanced over at the bar however, my mind immediately shifted to the task at hand.

Patricia sat at the bar, alone, nursing what looked like a whiskey on the rocks. Her slumped shoulders and the worried looks the bartending fairy kept shooting her told me she was not having a good night.

I motioned towards her to the others.

"We don't want to scare her off," Ellie suggested. "Amy, come with me. Let Sara and Tina talk to her."

Amy nodded, and the four of us split up, with Ellie and Amy making their way towards one of the booths on the right. Sara and I approached the bar and took the two seats immediately next to Patricia.

"Hey, Patricia, how are you doing?" Sara asked gently, and the Assistant looked up at us. Her eyes were bloodshot, and I was pretty sure it was from crying, since going by the amount of condensation on the glass and table, she'd been nursing that one drink for a while.

"Not great. I've just learned Philip's funeral is tomorrow. He really was a good guy."

"We heard he was fired from the hospital for stealing." Sara definitely got straight to the point. Patricia looked up suddenly from her drink.

"Where did you hear that?"

"Oh, it's just a rumor going around," Sara replied nonchalantly.

Patricia shook her head vehemently. "Not a chance. I knew Philip. And sure, he had his faults. He could be a little bit of a snoop, and he did drink too much, but he was a good guy. He was honest. He wouldn't have stolen anything."

"So he didn't tell you anything about it?" I asked.

"There was definitely nothing to tell. I can guarantee you that Philip did not steal from the hospital."

"We heard he was having money issues, though," Sara said.

Patricia nodded. "Sure. After all, it's not like being a general maintenance person for the hospital pays a whole bunch. Plus, Myrtle never worked if she could help it, so between the two of them they were definitely usually having money issues. But just because someone is poor doesn't mean they steal."

"No, of course not," I said quietly. "Do you know why he was fired from the hospital, if not for stealing?"

Patricia frowned. "No, I'm afraid I don't. To be honest, I didn't really speak with Philip in the past week. I did see him in the bar that night, and I thanked him when he bought the bar a round of drinks, but he seemed distracted somehow."

"Any idea why?"

Patricia shook her head. "No. I wish I did know. I wish he had confided in me. Then maybe we would know why he had been murdered. But, I really have no idea. All I can tell you is that on the night he murdered, Philip was in good spirits. He was happy."

"Thanks," Sara said quietly.

"Not a problem, anything I can do to help. But you have to believe me, Philip was no thief. He was a good man, he was an honest man. Now, I think this is probably my cue to go home. I managed to get tomorrow off so I could go to the funeral, and I'd like to get some rest before it starts."

Patricia settled up her tab, and I made my way back to the booths where the other two girls were sitting while Sara ordered drinks for all of us.

I repeated to Amy and Ellie what we had heard from Patricia.

"So she really has no idea what he could have stolen?" Amy said dejectedly when I finished.

"No, but I mean, what kind of guy is going to tell his friends that he was caught stealing at work and that's why he was fired? I kind of can't blame him for keeping that a secret."

Sara slipped into the booth as well, telling us that the waitress would be by shortly with our drinks.

"Someone else can drink mine, I have to get back to coven headquarters," Amy said.

"What did you tell Lita to get a couple of hours off?" Ellie asked.

"I told her I wanted to work with you for a little bit longer, to try and get your magic going. She thought that was an excellent idea, and told me to take a few hours off. But I really do need to get back; I know Lita has a whole bunch of papers that she wants help with."

Waving goodbye, Amy stepped out of the bar just as the waitress arrived with our drinks. She was a fairy as well, with her wings fluttering behind her, and I was surprised that she was able to hold up the tray with so many drinks given her small frame. She couldn't have been more than four and a half feet tall, and probably weighed eighty pounds, tops. Still, she balanced the tray on one arm with expert precision as she grabbed the drinks off of it and placed them on the table.

"I have four dragonberry juices for you ladies," she said. I looked at the glass placed in front of me in amazement. I had no idea what a dragonberry was, but this drink looked like a mixture of different colors, slowly melting together, each color twisting and winding around the others, almost like a multi-coloured lava lamp.

"Can I drink this?" I asked in amazement, looking at the drink.

"You must be the new witch in town," the fairy said with a smile. "Yes, you can drink it. Dragonberry juice is one of the most popular non-alcoholic drinks in town."

"I figured since the four of us have already demol-ished one and a half bottles of wine at home today, we should go for something a little bit less alcoholic, lest we all wake up hung over," Sara said with a smile.

"That was definitely a good choice," Ellie said. "Ailsa, why don't you join us? You can drink Amy's juice, since she had to leave."

"Well, seeing as it's a Tuesday night and we don't have that many customers, why not?" the fairy asked, fluttering her wings and slipping into the booth next to Ellie.

"I saw you chatting to Patricia," she said to Sara and I. "I assume you were talking to her about Philip?"

"How did you know?" I asked, slightly suspicious. I took a sip of the drink, and my eyes widened as my mouth burst with flavor. It was like eating some sort of fruit salad, where I had about five different flavors all at once. There was some sour citrus, a sweet berry taste, and a few others that I couldn't quite place. I was definitely a fan, though.

Ailsa gave me a wink and a smile. "Well, to be totally honest, I've heard the rumors that have linked your arrival with Philip's death. I don't believe them, of course, because that's totally ridiculous, but I have to say a decent number of the people in town actually believe you might've killed him. So, knowing that you are hanging out with Ellie here, I figured your little group is trying to figure out what happened to him. And Patricia is definitely one of the main people to speak to."

"That's true," Sara said. "We know that she and Philip were friends."

Ailsa giggled behind her hands. "Right. Friends."

"What do you mean?" Sara asked, leaning forward towards Ailsa.

"I've spent a lot of time in this bar, and I've seen a lot of witches and wizards. I know when something is going on between them, and something was *definitely* going on between Philip and Patricia. At least, until about a week ago, anyway."

"That jives with what she told us," I said slowly. "She said that Philip had been distant for the last week."

"If you ask me, the two of them broke up. But they were definitely together. They always tried to keep it subtle, and they never left together or arrived together, but I could see simply from the way they looked at each other that they were knocking boots," Ailsa said.

"Well, that suddenly opens up a new possibility," Ellie said. "If the two of them broke up about a week ago, then what if it was bad? What if Patricia actually did kill him out of jealousy, or simply anger for being dumped?"

"I don't know," I said slowly. "I think if it was her, she would have taken the opportunity to tell us that Philip was a thief, in the hopes of directing our energies elsewhere."

"That's true," Sara said. "Plus, she definitely was crying when we got to the bar."

"Yeah, but what if she wasn't crying out of grief? What if she was crying out of guilt, regretting the fact that she killed her ex?" Ellie suggested. "I don't think we can discount her completely. Do you know anything else about their breakup?"

Ailsa shook her head. "No, I don't. I know about a week ago they were sitting at a table at the back together, and while they were speaking in hushed tones, and I couldn't make out any of the words, it didn't look like a pleasant conversation. Eventually, Patricia left, and Philip had like five more drinks before staggering out of the bar himself an hour later."

"Great, so it doesn't sound like it was a very amicable breakup."

"No wonder she told us he had been distant," I said. "She couldn't exactly tell us that they were no longer an item. What I don't get, to be totally honest, is what someone like Patricia would have seen in a guy like Phillip. By all accounts he was basically a loser wizard going from dead-end job to dead-end job."

Ellie grinned at me. "You've never seen a picture of Philip, have you?"

I shook my head.

"The guy was basically the hottest wizard in town. Even though he was in his early forties, the guy was incredibly good looking. I was honestly surprised that he didn't go try his luck in Spellywood; he probably could have gotten at least a few gigs."

"So he was basically the George Clooney of the paranormal world," I nodded.

"Who's George Clooney?" Ailsa asked.

"Just ignore her, she's always making references to the human world that none of us understand," Sara said good-naturedly, sticking her tongue out at me.

"Yeah, well, George Clooney is super-hot," I replied. "That's all you really need to know. That explains it, anyway. I guess I just never envisioned the hospital maintenance guy to be good looking."

"Oh, he was," Sara confirmed. "It wasn't just the

moon he was connected to which was fiery," she added with a wink.

"Did Myrtle know?" I asked. "After all, his wife may not have been super happy about the affair."

Ailsa shrugged. "I have no idea. She doesn't come in here much; I think I've only seen her once or twice since I started working here a couple of years ago."

"Thanks for the info. That really helps."

"Not a problem. And don't worry about paying for those drinks. Consider it our welcome to Western Woods, Tina."

"Thanks," I said, a small blush rose on my face. It was really nice to see that most of the community was actually quite welcoming. I had a feeling the adjustment to the paranormal world would be a lot easier with most people on my side.

"Right. I've got to get going, since I am still on the clock, but I do hope that someone finds out who the murderer is, whether it be you or Chief Enforcer King."

"Thanks, Ailsa," Ellie said. "It was nice to see you again."

"You too. See you, witches."

As Ailsa left, the three of us sipped our drinks in silence, all of us thinking over what we had just learned. We might not have learned what Philip had stolen from the hospital which got him fired, but we certainly did have one, possibly two new suspects.

CHAPTER 18

I spent most of that night tossing and turning, mulling over in my head everything we had learned about Philip Vulcan's death. Eventually, when the first rays of sunlight began to shine through the window, I gave up on the idea of sleep and got out of bed.

"Finally," Mr. Meowgi muttered, crawling into the warm spot I had left and curling up into a ball. "Some of us have been trying to sleep."

"Sorry," I whispered to him softly, giving him a quick pat on the head. Slipping into my clothes, I made my way into the kitchen, where I found Ellie eating a piece of toast while Chestnut sat at her feet, staring intently at the bread, as if he could make it drop if he stared hard enough.

"Use the force, Chestnut," I said to him softly, but he

was so focused on the bread he didn't pay me any attention.

"Another human reference?" Ellie asked, and I nodded as I made my way to the fridge.

"Do we have any of that dragonberry juice?" I asked, peering through the fridge. "That stuff was good."

Ellie grinned. "Sadly, no. I think Amy's going shopping this afternoon though, so if you leave a note on the fridge she'll buy some for you."

"Where is Amy, anyway?"

"Sleeping, I think. Even with that potion that lets her stay up, she does need to sleep occasionally."

"It's good to see that even she's human – er, a witch."

Ellie laughed. "Absolutely. Anyway, I'm going to work soon. Hexpresso Bean is catering the funeral, which is at eleven. I assume the three of you will be there?"

"Yes, for sure. After all, I'm part of this coven now, and I definitely want to go to the coven events. Although, it would be nice if the next one wasn't a funeral."

"I agree with you there," Ellie said. "Anyway, take care of yourself. There will be people at the funeral who think you killed him, don't pay them any mind. Those people are idiots."

And with that, Ellie got up and placed her plate in the sink, before waving her wand at it.

"*In the name of hygiene, make these dishes clean.*"

A second later the plate glimmered as though it was brand-new. I gasped; magic was still definitely new, and definitely cool. There was no way my old Maytag could compete with that.

"I thought all of the spells had to invoke Jupiter," I said. "That spell didn't include him at all."

"Most do," Ellie said with a shrug. "But not all of them. I think for the spell makers it became pretty awkward if they had to try and rhyme everything with Jupiter somehow."

"So is that a spell that I can do, and it won't be weaker because it's not the spell of my coven?"

Ellie shook her head. "Sadly, no. Even spells that don't directly invoke our celestial spirit are coven specific."

I sighed. I was definitely going to have to try and figure out who my coven was sooner rather than later.

After Ellie – and Chestnut - left, I picked up one of the books I'd bought at the bookstore before leaving – *The Complete Collection of Sherlock Holmes* – and curled up on the couch, reading away, until about half an hour later Sara came out of her room, arms outstretched, in the middle of a yawn.

"Just the two of us this morning, hey?"

"Apparently, Amy is sleeping," I replied with a smile.

"Huh, that's a first," Sara said, grabbing an apple from the fruit bowl on the kitchen island and biting into it. "Well, it's only seven, and the funeral doesn't start until eleven, so we have lots of time until then to give you your first broom lesson, if you're up for it."

My heart leapt into my throat at Sara's words – partly from excitement, and partly out of fear. I had never been particularly athletic when I was in school, and I worried that would show itself in my broom riding abilities. Or, more accurately, my lack of them.

Still, this was going to happen! I was going to learn how to ride a broom. A real broom.

"Sure," I said, trying to sound casual, but given as it came out as a bit of a squeak, Sara grinned at me.

"A bit nervous?"

"Just a tad," I replied.

"Don't worry. It's not actually hard, and the brooms are magically designed to keep you on them. It's not like you're going to fall off if you shift your weight over three inches."

"That's a relief," I noted. That was what worried me the most about broom riding: that I was going to need absolutely perfect balance. I had trouble walking in high-heeled shoes; I could imagine that a broom ride was just *asking* for disaster.

"Come on, let's get going."

"Don't you want to have breakfast first?" I offered.

"Nah, I'm not that hungry. And besides, why would I eat breakfast when I finally have the opportunity to teach another witch something?" she added with a wink.

Grabbing the smaller broom from the pile of four at

the side of the house – Ellie hadn't taken her broom to work today, apparently – Sara motioned for me to follow her into the backyard. It was definitely big, at least by city standards – probably about fifty feet deep, and spanning about fifteen feet on either side of the house. "There's lots of room here for you to practice," Sara said, motioning around the yard.

I was pleased to see the yard was well-manicured, but plain. Apart from a small set of bushes against the back fence, there was only grass. No large trees or anything like that for me to accidentally fly into.

"Now, the most important thing to remember when you're flying is not to panic. Panic is what causes problems. If you stay calm, no matter what happens, your broom will stay stable, and you're more likely to get yourself out of a bad situation. Besides, you're basically never going to find yourself in a bad situation anyway. Ninety-nine percent of the flying that you do is going to be to get from shop to shop in town. It's rather low risk."

"What about the other one percent?"

Sara grinned. "Well, seeing as it took very little convincing for you to break into the hospital with us last night, I have a feeling you're going to be more into adventures than Amy is."

"Not a chance. Once this is over, I plan on living a quiet life as I learn what it's like to be a witch."

"Alright, well, one of the most important parts of being a witch is knowing how to fly a broom. So, the first thing you need to know how to do is set a broom straight. Pick it up, hold it horizontally just under hip height, and let it go. If you focus on the broom while you're doing it, the broom will float next to you so you can get on. Just like this."

Sara did exactly as she'd just explained, and when she let go of the broom, it held in place. I let out a small gasp of wonder. That was cool!

"Now you try."

I made my way over to the broom and picked it up. As soon as I touched it, the magical link with Sara ended, and it fell limply into my hand.

"Ok," I muttered, thinking about the broom as I held it about halfway up my thigh. What kind of broom was this, anyway? Would this work with any broom?

I let go, but to my dismay, the broom simply fell on the ground.

"Were you thinking about the broom?" Sara asked, motioning for me to pick it up.

"Um, well, I was thinking about brooms in general," I admitted, biting my lip.

"You need to focus on this broom, in the same way as you focus on your wand when you do a spell. Ok? Try again."

This time, I really tried to mimic how I focused on the wand with the broom, and when I let go of it, rather than falling limply to the ground, the broom hovered where I'd left it. It felt like there was an energy between me and the broom, like we were connected somehow.

"Great!" Sara said, clapping her hands together with a grin.

"That's awesome," I said, staring at the broom. I still wasn't over the novelty of how cool magic was.

"Now, the next step is to get on the broom, and learn to fly," Sara said. "I'll be right back."

She came back a second later with her own broom. "Ok, I'm going to show you on this one. Basically, you sit down on the broom, which you learned to do yesterday. When you're on it, hold onto the front with both hands. The front of the broom acts like the steering mechanism. If you want to go up, you pull up on the broom. If you want to go down, you push down on it. If you want to go faster, shift your weight forward over the front of the broom, and if you want to slow down, shift your weight towards the back. Got it?"

I nodded. "I think so."

"It's really actually fairly intuitive once you get going. And of course, to turn, you simply steer your shoulders in the direction you want to go."

"Alright. So, uh, do you want me to try that now?"

"There's really no other way."

"No training wheels on brooms, hey?"

"Why would brooms come with wheels?" Sara asked, her head tilting to the side.

"Never mind," I muttered. Hoisting myself over the

broom's handle, I let my feet just tickle the ground slightly. I liked having that connection, at least to start.

"Good. Now, hands firmly on the front, and shift your weight forward just a little bit," Sara urged.

I did as she said, and as soon as I shifted my weight to the front of the broom, it began to move. I gasped and moved back instinctively, and the broom stopped.

"See? Nothing to worry about," Sara said. "Why did you pull back?"

"Instinct," I replied. "Ok, let me try again."

This time, when I leaned my weight forward over the broom, I was expecting it to go forward, and when it did, while my heart rate increased noticeably, I didn't panic, and instead simply gripped the front of the broom more tightly.

I mean, I was probably moving at approximately two miles an hour, but still. Baby steps.

"Good!" Sara called out encouragingly. "That's how you do it!"

As I rode slowly through the backyard, my confidence level began to grow. I even began to smile as I lifted the broom about a foot higher, so my feet could no longer touch the ground, and I continued to do small circles around the backyard.

"Excellent, you're really getting the hang of this!" Sara said excitedly. She was obviously enjoying my success as much as I was, and it was really nice to see someone being so happy for me when in reality I was still very much a beginner.

As I continued to zip around the backyard - okay, zip was probably a strong word - I began to feel like maybe I could actually do this. Maybe I wasn't going to be the worst witch ever after all.

"Oh, a broom, where are we going?" I heard a familiar voice call out from somewhere behind me. The next thing I knew, a black ball of fur was running towards me, and a second later had jumped up onto the back of the broom. Mr. Meowgi was obviously not going to be left out this time.

The extra weight on the back made the front part of the broom handle rise, which led to the broom immediately soaring upwards. This was definitely a lot higher than I had ever expected to go, and a lot higher than I was comfortable with.

"Eek," I cried as I began to panic. The one thing Sara had told me not to do. In my fear, I leaned forward to hug the broom handle to get a better grip on it, but all that did was make the broom rise faster.

"Never mind, I'm out of here, you have no idea how to ride one of these things," my familiar said, leaping off the back of the broom and landing daintily on the ground, which was now at least twenty feet below.

"Stop panicking," Sara called out from the ground below. It was easy for her to say. She wasn't the one climbing steadily on a broom she'd only just learned to ride that morning.

On the other hand, I knew that if I didn't want to end up in space, I was eventually going to have to pull back. It took every ounce of willpower in my being, but I eventually pulled myself back from the broom handle, and leveled out the broom.

Shifting my weight backwards, as Sara had told me, I slowed the broom down considerably, until I was just barely crawling through the air. I really hoped brooms weren't like helicopters, where if they stopped they would just drop out of the sky. But so far, everything about this ride seemed to defy physics, and I was still floating. So, I figured I was doing okay.

"Good," Sara called out. "Way to get a hold of it. Now, come back down."

I looked down at the ground, and my heart lurched in my chest. I had to be at least sixty feet high. My feet dangled underneath the broom, with nothing but air between them and the hard grass below.

I had never been afraid of heights, but I figured this fell into a whole different category. I tried to press down on the broom handle and bring the broom back to earth, but I quickly found that my body had decided it wasn't cooperating with me anymore. Instead, I was frozen. I couldn't move. I was just so scared that anything I would do would lead straight to me plummeting to the earth.

"Tina? Come on down. You can do this," Sara called out to me. Nope. My brain definitely did not agree.

In the distance, a black dot appeared. It was far away to start with, but as I got closer, I realized it was a dragon. My fear momentarily forgotten, I sat transfixed on my broom, watching as the dragon came closer and closer towards us. Was this Drake?

The wings of the dragon beat with an elegance and grace that was hard to describe. It was like watching a mid-air dance, and even as he got closer and closer towards me, until I could see that he was not only black, but with a chest covered in blue and white scales, I couldn't stop watching him. It definitely couldn't be Drake; his scales had been red, orange, and yellow.

"Tina? You have to come down here," Sara said, panic rising in her voice this time. "There's a dragon coming. Why is he here? They know they're not allowed to shift during the day."

I didn't know the rules and regulations around dragon shifting, but as he got to within a hundred feet of me, suddenly panic gripped me once more. The dragon was really coming directly at me. Was I about to be eaten?

The answer was a lot worse. The dragon flew straight past me, and the air from his powerful wings knocked me sideways. I let out a cry as I slipped from the broom, hanging on to it with just my hands, dangling in midair.

"Oh my God," Sara said. "I'm coming up to get you. Hold on."

"There's no time," I shouted at her, my brain evidently deciding to work again. "I'm losing my grip."

It didn't help that I had the upper body strength of a

toddler. This was definitely it. This is how I was going to die.

"Okay, I'll use a spell," Sara said. "I'm going to make an air bag for you to fall onto."

"Hurry!" I shouted just as my grip gave up and I fell from the broom, plummeting toward the ground.

I screamed and closed my eyes as I hurtled back towards the earth, hoping desperately that Sara's spell would work. At the very last second, I opened my eyes, determined that if this was going to be my last moment on earth I would at least see it, only to find myself looking straight into a giant pool of water.

I just had time to hold my breath a split second before I hit the water with a splash, my body cocooned by the cold water's embrace.

A few seconds later, after kicking back to the surface, I wiped the water out of my eyes to find myself staring directly at an incredibly relieved looking Sara.

"Oh thank Jupiter," she said. "I'm so glad you're okay."

Looking around, it turned out that Sara had turned the entire backyard into a giant pool. She stood on the edge, about a three foot wide gap between the edge of the new pool and the door to the house.

"I'm not sure the others are going to like your choice of redecorating," I said, and Sara let out a half hysterical laugh.

"I tried to make an air bag. I really did, but this

happened instead. I don't know how, but this is always what happens when I try to use spells."

"Hey, I'm not lying dead in the middle of a patch of grass; as far as I'm concerned, your spell did what it was supposed to. Now, what on earth was a dragon doing in the middle of the sky, and why didn't you warn me that could happen?"

Sara shook her head. "I have no idea. We need to report this to the head of the shifters. They're not supposed to shift during the day. They have to do it at night, when there is very little risk of any interfering broom traffic. For exactly reasons like this."

I climbed out of the makeshift pool and found Mr. Meowgi running back into the house. Evidently, his martial arts skills didn't extend to falling victim to a few drops of water on his fur.

"Sure, but I might go inside and get dried off first."

CHAPTER 19

"I can't believe you just jumped onto my broom like that," I said to my familiar, who sat on the bed while I towel dried my hair after changing into something dry.

"How was I supposed to know you had no idea how to ride a broom?"

"Wasn't it obvious?"

"I thought you were just getting started, and I didn't want to miss anything. So, I jumped on. No one told me that I was getting a witch who didn't know how to be a witch."

"Yeah, well, now you know," I grumbled as I ran a brush through my hair, pulling at a couple of knots that had formed during the course of my adventure.

"Can I at least come with you to see the shifters?" Mr. Meowgi asked.

"Fine, but you have to behave."

"Hey, I'm not the one who just fell sixty feet off a broom today."

I shot my cat a look.

"Fine, fine," he replied. "I promise to behave."

Sara and I dressed in black - well, dressed in one of Randy's magical outfits, which changed color based on the occasion. We had decided that we would go straight from shifter headquarters to the funeral.

"I can come to the funeral as well. I'm already dressed for it," Mr. Meowgi bragged, and I shot him a sly look out of the corner of my eye.

"Again, only if you behave."

"Of course. I will be the picture of obedience."

I highly doubted that, but despite all the red flags decided that my familiar could come along after all. He seemed very excited about meeting the shifters.

I didn't really know where I expected the shifters to be headquartered. Anything from a mansion to a cave would have seemed appropriate to me, so when Sara and I made our way to a large, Gothic building that reminded me more of a medieval church than a group headquarters, I wasn't entirely surprised.

Sara knocked on the large wooden doors, which opened almost immediately to reveal a young shifter, probably about my age, with a long nose and round eyes. I frowned slightly; I didn't know what kind of shifter he could be.

"Hello, what brings two witches to the shifters lair?"

"We need to speak with Mr. Lupo," Sara replied. "It's important."

"*I* decide if something is important enough to speak to Mr. Lupo about," the man replied, standing tall and doing his best to look important.

"I assure you, this is a very private matter. And I can also assure you that Mr. Lupo will not be happy if you turn us away when we need to tell him something that pertains to the safety of his shifters."

Apparently, the way to fight posturing with shifters was more posturing. Sara's approach worked, and after a moment, the young shifter opened the door for us.

"You had better not be lying to me," he growled, and it came to me then. Wolf. This guy had to be a wolf shifter.

I tried not to look around in awe as we passed into the main part of the shifters' lair. It really did look like a church, but without any pews, and funnily enough it reminded me a little bit of the coven headquarters. For all of this separation, the different paranormals here really did have a lot in common.

The walls were lined with portraits and photos of former shifters, and I spotted one who bore a very familiar resemblance to Drake. I made a mental note to ask him about it the next time I saw him.

The young wolf shifter led us to the center of the building, where the altar would have been if this had been a church. Instead, a wall had been built, all the way up the at least thirty feet to the ceiling. A dark cherry door gilded with gold led into this space, and the wolf knocked before entering, motioning for Sara and me to follow.

To Mr. Meowgi's credit, he walked next to me in silence, for once.

"Two witches to see you, sir. They won't state their business, but claim it's important."

"Well, then by all means, show them in," I heard a voice reply from the other side of the door. The young wolf shifter stepped aside to let us through to speak to the head of the shifters, and as soon as he did my breath caught in my throat.

I had expected the leader of such a pack to be an older shifter, someone who had been around for a while and had long since established his dominance.

Instead, I found myself staring into the eyes of one of the most gorgeous men I'd ever seen. His long, blond hair flowed to his shoulders, and his eyes were a light brown color that shone in the light. The simple polo shirt he wore showed off his tanned skin and muscular physique, and I knew instinctively that this man was a lion shifter.

"Oh my goodness, this is a living God among cats," Mr. Meowgi said, obviously impressed. I couldn't say I disagreed.

"Witches, welcome. What can I do for you?" he asked, motioning for us to sit on a couple of comfortable-looking chairs in the middle of the room. He had a desk, but rather than sit on it, he spread himself out on a large couch against the wall, draping his arm over the back of it and looking casually over at us.

Definitely not what I had expected.

"Hi, Mr. Lupo," Sara started.

"Please, call me Jackson."

"Er, um, yes." It was obvious she was nervous. "We came here today because we needed to tell you about an incident in our yard this morning."

"Yes?"

"Well, you see, Tina here, she's a new witch in town."

"Ah, so this is our new arrival. Welcome," he said to me, sending a blush shooting straight up my face. Great. Now I probably looked like a tomato, on top of a drowned rat.

"Thanks," I stammered, like a freaking six year old. Just because this guy was basically an Adonis didn't mean I had to panic every time he even looked at me.

"I was teaching her how to ride a broom this morning in our yard. Unfortunately, Tina panicked a little bit and got stuck at a significant height. This would have been fine, as I could have gone up to get her, except that a dragon appeared and flew close to her, the wind from its wings blowing her off the broom. I managed to turn our backyard into a pool, which broke her fall, but obviously the fact that this incident happened at all is pretty serious. We came straight here."

Jackson's demeanor went straight from casual to

serious. He stood up and made his way behind his desk, where he opened a notepad and grabbed a pen. "You're completely right," he said. "That's absolutely unacceptable. Thank you for bringing this to my attention. Tina, I apologize on behalf of the shifter community. This never should have happened to you, and I'm so glad to hear you're alright."

"No problem," I squeaked.

"Now, can you tell me anything about the dragon that flew near you?"

"Um, it was mainly black, but the scales on its chest were kind of blue and white, and they glimmered in the sun," I said. "And it was big. That's all I can tell you, sorry."

"No, that's helpful," Jackson nodded. "I'm reasonably certain I know who was behind this. I will make sure he is punished, as flying during the day is completely unacceptable, and flying near the new witch in town even less so."

"I suspect he was trying to scare Tina," Sara offered up, and Jackson nodded.

"I think that is likely."

"What?" I said, my mouth drying up. I had thought the dragon did it by accident. This was on *purpose?*

"A lot of the shifters think you killed Philip," Sara said. "We've been trying to keep you away from anyone who believes it, but I wouldn't be surprised if the dragon was just trying to send you a message."

"I agree with Sara. He probably didn't realize that

you were such an amateur on the broom and didn't expect you to fall off completely. Not that it excuses his behavior, not in the least. But I suspect that was the intent: to scare you."

"Great," I said, staring down at the ground. Not only was I totally new to this world, but there were already people here trying to drive me out of it. Tears threatened to sting my eyes, and I blinked hard.

"Hey," Sara said softly, putting a hand on my arm. "It's ok. Not everyone thinks like those idiots, most people here know that you're not the murderer."

"Exactly," Jackson added with a firm nod. "I promise you that most of the shifter community believes in your innocence. After all, what possible reason could a newcomer here have to commit murder straight away? I will make sure that the dragon shifter who did this to you is punished. I will speak with Chief Enforcer King about this and make sure that it never happens again."

"Thanks," I said, giving Jackson a small smile. It was nice of him to say that, and I was glad that he at least didn't think I'd killed Philip.

"Now this is a leader," Mr. Meowgi nodded from his spot at my feet. "You should pay attention to Mr. Lupo here. He obviously knows how to lead a pack."

I smiled at Mr. Meowgi, who was obviously super impressed by the lion shifter. I supposed for a small domestic shorthaired cat like him, the big lion must have been super impressive.

Sara stood up, and I followed her cue. "Thanks, Jackson."

"Not a problem, witches. Thank you for coming to me with this, I appreciate it. I cannot keep my people in line if I don't know there is an issue, and I promise you, this will be dealt with appropriately."

Sara and I left, and were immediately led back outside by the young wolf shifter.

As soon as we stepped outside, Sara turned to me and smiled. "See? That wasn't so bad, was it? Also, Mr. Lion Shifter in there *totally* has a thing for you."

"What? No way, that's ridiculous," I said, the blush creeping back up my face.

"No, he does. I mean, it's not like you're going to be the love of his life or anything: being a shifter, he's going to have to marry another lion shiftress, lest he be kicked out of his pack. But, still. I think he likes you."

"That's ridiculous," I muttered. "You guys really do have a lot of rules about intermingling between different paranormal species, hey?"

"Well, the shifters are a lot more serious about it than most, but that's also in part because they're a lot more insular than most paranormal species. I mean sure, we have the coven and all, but even I can admit that the shifter pack is much closer than all of us witches. I mean, I don't even know some of the younger coven witches. And genetically, if a shifter has a baby with a non-shifter, the non-shifter's powers are the ones which the baby receives, generally. There's only one exception: if a wizard has a baby with a shiftress, the baby will be a shifter, since the witch gene is passed through the mother."

"Still, it seems really insular."

"Yeah, it is. But don't worry, you'll get used to it."

Would I? It was one thing to like hanging out with your own group of people, but everything here seemed so unnecessarily regimented.

"Anyway, we have to get going to the funeral, it's almost eleven."

CHAPTER 20

To be honest, I had actually naturally expected the funeral to take place in some sort of magical church. After all, this was where funerals took place.

That's why, when Sara led me to a large, open garden, I was a little bit surprised.

"Is this where it's happening?" I asked.

Sara nodded. "This is the coven gardens, where every important ceremony that involves witches or wizards takes place."

I had to admit, it was absolutely gorgeous. Large, manicured lawns spread out as far as the eye could see, with meandering paths making their way through the space. Large trees offered plenty of shade from the summer sun, and a small river snaked through the center of the space, leading to a large lake in the middle of the park. Magical fountains spurted water as they moved around the lake, enchanted. This was definitely the kind of place where I could spend a lazy summer afternoon, lying on a blanket, engrossed in a book.

Sara and I followed one path towards the lake in the center. Along one side of the lake was a large gathering of people, and I assumed this was where the funeral was going to take place.

At one end, a large table was set up, filled with plenty of food and drink. I spotted Ellie bustling around, and as she caught my eye she gave me a quick wave before getting back to her work.

"Is Amy going to be here?" I asked, and Sara nodded.

"She texted me about half an hour ago, wanting to know where we were. I told her we would meet her here, so shout out if you see her."

"Are all of these people from the coven?"

"No, while some coven ceremonies are private, funerals are not, and anyone from the town who would like to pay their respects is able to do so. So not only did Philip have some non-coven friends in town, but a lot of people are going to be here simply out of idle curiosity. It's been a long time since we've had anyone murdered here in town."

As Sara kept an eye out for Amy, I looked around as well, but I was almost more focused on the other people around. After all, I still knew very few of the people who lived here in Western Woods, and I was curious. Near the edge of the lake, a plump woman with curly blonde hair and a fancy black dress cried into a handkerchief. She was being comforted by a man in robes who I assumed was the priest - or whatever the magical equivalent was - and I had to assume that this was Myrtle, Philip's wife.

About twenty feet away from Myrtle stood Patricia, tall, stoic, and looking completely alone. Even though she was a homewrecker, by all accounts, I had to feel a little bit sorry for her. She was obviously grieving as well, though I couldn't help but wonder if she had been the one to put Philip here. After all, he had broken up with her just before he was killed.

Among all of the other unfamiliar faces were a few that I recognized. Randy Tonner was there, along with his husband Eric. Caranthir stood at least a foot taller than almost everybody else, the elegant elf looking suitably somber for the occasion. Sara's mother and her fiery red hair stood out as well; she was speaking with Caranthir and a couple of others, one of whom still had her triangular badge on. This was obviously the group of Philip's former coworkers.

"Oh, there's Amy," Sara said suddenly, grabbing my arm. The two of us made our way towards her, and she smiled when she saw us.

"Hey, how's it going?"

"Good, thanks," I answered.

"Cool. Hey, do either one of you know why the backyard has been turned into a lake?"

Sara and I looked at each other. "It's a long story," I replied. "We'll tell you later."

Just then, the priest stood up on a makeshift stage that I assumed had been conjured just then, as it wasn't there when I had seen him a few moments earlier.

He pointed at his throat with his wand, muttering a few words, and when he spoke a few seconds later, his voice was amplified, as though he was using a microphone.

"Witches, wizards, and all magical creatures. I please welcome you to take a seat, as we will begin our celebration of Philip Vulcan's life shortly."

A buzz came up from the crowd as everyone began to mill around, trying to find a place to sit. Sara, Amy, and I found a patch of cool grass on a bit of a hill a few feet away, which allowed us to see everything, even though we were pretty far from shore. Eventually, when everybody was seated, the priest raised his arms, indicating for everybody to be quiet. His bald head practically glowed in the sun's glare, and I imagined that he must have been quite hot in the heavy-looking robes he wore.

"Welcome, and let me begin by thanking all of you for coming to celebrate the life of one of Western Woods' great magical citizens. As many of you know, I am the Oracle of Jupiter. Philip Vulcan may not have been born here, but he moved here for love, and I know from speaking with him that he was always touched by the way the people of this great town welcomed him as one of their own. Even though he was not guided by Jupiter, as most of the rest of us are, he fit in well in this coven, and we accepted him as family."

The Oracle continued on for about ten minutes, speaking about Philip Vulcan and his life, and the impact he had on the people who lived here. Afterwards, his wife Myrtle got up to speak. She managed to keep it together, and I couldn't help but wonder if maybe *she* was the killer, rather than Patricia. Had she known about the affair and killed Philip in a jealous rage?

"Now, in the tradition of his original coven, the good witches and wizards guided by the celestial being Io, please join me in sending Philip Vulcan's body back to the skies. I will ask everybody to stand for the ceremony."

A small murmur ran through the crowd; evidently, I wasn't the only one who didn't know what was going to happen now.

"What does Io's coven do for funerals?" I whispered to Sara, who shrugged.

Amy shot her a look. "You really should have read more books in the library when we were at the Academy," she said. "Many of the celestial covens ruled by fire use funeral pyres. In the case of the coven of Io, the pyre has to take place over water."

So we were about to see the magical version of a Viking funeral. I had to admit, that was pretty cool.

Sure enough, the Oracle stepped off the stage, and with a wave of his wand and a muttering of a spell, the stage disappeared to reveal a boat about seven feet long and two feet wide. It was completely encased, like a coffin.

Two wizards that I didn't recognize stepped up to the boat. One of them held an old-fashioned torch, whose flames leapt high in the summer breeze. They held hands, and one of the men placed the torch on top of the boat, before both of them pushed it into the lake.

There had to be some sort of accelerant on the wood, because the boat caught fire immediately. Flames and smoke rose high up into the air, the crackling of the flames mingling with Myrtle's sobs as her husband's body drifted out towards the center of the lake.

For about three minutes everyone stood in silence, except for the sounds of crying, until finally the wooden boat and the body had been completely engulfed in flames and it all petered out without so much as a sound. Smoke continued to rise from the lake, but Philip Vulcan's body was gone.

"I thank you all for coming to the ceremony," the Oracle said about thirty seconds after the last of the flames had been extinguished. "Please stay as long as you would like to celebrate the life of Philip Vulcan. There is food, and refreshments."

With that, everyone began to talk once more, the low hum of voices passing over the crowd.

"That was incredible," Amy said, her eyes glimmering. "I'd heard of the funeral rites of many of the fire covens, but to see one in person was just something else."

"I thought it was quite touching," Sara said.

I nodded in agreement as the three of us made our way towards the large number of tables containing food. I hadn't noticed before, but there were now at least a dozen of them, all with delicious pastries and plenty of drink dispensers.

"Do you think they'll have Dragonberry juice?" I asked, looking around.

"For sure, it's over there," Sara said. "I'm going to go get some of this delicious food, after all, I skipped breakfast this morning."

The three of us separated as we weaved our way around the groups of people munching away and chatting idly. I grabbed my juice, and made my way away from the crowd, before spotting Chief Enforcer King standing by herself under a tree, overlooking the group of people.

Making my way towards her, she smiled as she saw me coming.

"Tina? How are you settling in?"

"Great, thanks," I told her. "There have been a few challenges, what with some of the people in town thinking I killed Philip, but for the most part it's been great." I joined her under the tree, and as I stared over the crowd, I couldn't help but notice my familiar standing directly underneath the table featuring what looked like shrimp. I had completely lost track of Mr. Meowgi, but it was good to see he was fending for himself, as he did his best to look like a pathetic cat who definitely had not been fed breakfast that morning and who was absolutely starving. I made a mental note to keep an eye on him; I didn't want him to get bolder and start stealing food directly off the table.

Chief Enforcer King nodded. "I've heard the rumors as well. It's disappointing to say the least."

"Do you have any idea who actually killed Philip?" I asked.

"I'm afraid I can't speak about an open investigation at all."

"Oh. Right, sorry."

"Not to worry. You're certainly not the first person to ask me that. With murder being so rare here in Western Woods, I think the whole town is both a little bit on edge, and also taken in simply by morbid curiosity."

"I think you're right," I said, motioning around. "After all, I don't think all of these people were Philip's best friends."

Chief Enforcer King laughed. "You've got that right. Now, if you'll excuse me, I wanted to have a little bit of a chat with Patricia Trovao."

"Sure. Nice to see you," I said.

"You too. See you around." I watched as Chief Enforcer King walked away from the tree and made her way towards Patricia. Did she suspect her of murder as well? Did she know about the affair? There were so many questions, and I just didn't know how to answer them.

I watched closely, unable to listen in, as Chief Enforcer King spoke with Patricia. It certainly didn't look like an interrogation to me; in fact, if I hadn't known that this was the head of law enforcement for the town, I would have thought that it was just a conversation between two friends. They seemed quite friendly, as though they were just having a conversation. Maybe they were. After all, what did I know about Chief Enforcer King's methods?

"Enjoying the view?" a familiar voice said at my side, and my heart skipped a beat as I looked over to see Kyran standing there, grinning away.

CHAPTER 21

"*I* thought you were in the hospital!"

"One of the cool things about being an elf, not only are we immortal, but when we don't die we heal a lot faster than you genetically inferior witches," he added with a wink.

"So you're okay then," I said, my eyes immediately going to Kyran's mid-section, which was covered by a T-shirt so tight it didn't even come close to hiding the fact that he was extremely fit.

"Never better. Though the Healers at the hospital did help with that. And how about you? Not having too much trouble here in town are you?"

I didn't know why, but I found myself telling Kyran all about the Dragon who knocked me off my broom. After all, hadn't all of my friends warned me against this guy? I shouldn't even have been talking to him, let alone telling him what had happened.

As I told the story, his face darkened. "Have you told Lupo about it?"

I nodded. "Sara took me to see him straight away."

"Good. Let me know if the problem is not solved to your satisfaction, as I'm pretty sure I know which dragon shifter it was."

"Who was it?" I asked, curious.

"The same one who did this to me," Kyran said with a wry smile. "He thinks the rules don't apply to him, because his father is one of the overseeing Senators for the shifter race in the paranormal world."

"Great. So not only did he knock me off my broom, but his dad's important."

"Yeah. Sometimes he gets away with things that he shouldn't. So, as I said, let me know if you ever have any trouble with him."

A part of me was actually afraid to ask what Kyran was going to do about it if he did get involved. After all, the guy had just gotten burned by the same guy - quite literally.

"Thanks," I just said. "I appreciate it."

"Not a problem. Can I get you some more drag-onberry juice?"

I accepted and watched as Kyran made his way through the crowd. I couldn't help but notice a number of the paranormal community making way for him as he passed, almost as if they were afraid of him. I couldn't understand why; as far as I was concerned, Kyran was a totally nice guy.

When he came back with the juice a couple of minutes later, I took it happily. "This is my favorite part of the paranormal world so far," I said.

Kyran laughed. "You have the ability to do spells to do almost anything, you can fly on a broom, and you can make potions that make you feel almost anything, and yet *dragonberry juice* is your favorite part of life here?"

I nodded. "I suppose you could say my life is a bit food oriented."

"So you're basically Liz Lemon."

I gasped. "A human world reference! You've seen *30 Rock*?"

Kyran grinned. "I told you, I spend a lot of time there chasing away paranormals trying to stir up trouble. I can't say I've seen every episode, but I've seen enough."

"And do you know *Harry Potter*?"

"Of course I do."

I laughed. "Finally, *someone* in this place might actually understand my references."

"Oh, you'll be making magical ones soon enough, I'm sure."

"Speaking of magic, what kind of magical powers do elves have? You said you're immortal, is that all?"

"It's not all, no. And despite our immortality, we can be killed."

"Like in *Lord of the Rings*."

"Exactly like that. And we do have magical powers,

although they aren't quite as obvious as yours. Elves have a very intuitive kind of magic. We're able to sense things that other creatures can't. It was how I knew as soon as I saw you that you were the new arrival in town."

"Ok," I nodded. "But so, you can't do spells, or anything like that?"

"Not in the way you're thinking. We are connected to the earth, however. If I wanted to create a thunderstorm right now, I could do that. Or, I could make the level of the lake rise. But I couldn't conjure up a cupcake right now."

"Well then what's even the point of having magical powers?" I asked, and Kyran laughed.

"Alright, well, that's my quota for interaction with people in town met for the day. I'm going to head off."

A part of me wanted to ask him why everyone seemed to avoid him as best they could, but I didn't want to be totally crass.

"What made you come here in the first place? Did you know Philip?"

"Saw him in the hospital a few times, but no, I didn't know him at all. I just came for the potential drama, but it looks like this is going to be a much more well-behaved wake than I had hoped for."

I wasn't entirely sure if Kyran was joking or not. "Anyway, I'll see you around."

"For sure," I said, watching as Kyran headed away from the lake and back towards the town.

I turned to see if I could catch a glimpse of Amy and Sara, but I assumed they had found other people to talk to themselves, as I couldn't spot them in the crowd at all.

"Well, might as well get a bit of food," I muttered to myself as my stomach grumbled. After all, I hadn't had any breakfast either. I found my familiar still happily begging for food under the shrimp table.

"You know, that breakfast you fed me really didn't feel like enough food," I heard a voice underneath me say.

"Oh, really?" I asked Mr. Meowgi, giving him a sly look as he peered up at me from the ground, giving me his best begging face. "And I'm sure you haven't been sitting here begging the entire time."

"Of course not, do I look like a cat who would shamelessly ask for food from strangers?"

"You absolutely do."

"Well, I never," Mr. Meowgi huffed in false outrage, and I laughed. I threw him a piece of shrimp, which he happily devoured, when I suddenly overheard a snippet of conversation between the people next to me.

"Oh, yes, well Myrtle knew all about it, you know."

My eyes widened as I looked over at who was speaking. It was a witch, for sure, speaking with another witch, but I didn't recognize either one of them. Although seeing as one of them wore one of the hospital badges with an H on it, I knew she had to be a witch Healer.

I stepped away from the table, turning my back to the two witches, trying to look like I was just casually eating some food instead of eavesdropping on their conversation.

"I just can't believe it. Myrtle had always been so independent. You know, her parents never wanted her to marry outside of the coven to begin with."

"I know. It's such a shame. She used to be so independent. And yet, Philip and Patricia were quite close to one another. I think it was more than friendship, personally."

The other witch made a tutting sound. "I imagine that's why Caranthir had Philip fired."

"Goodness, I haven't the slightest. I imagine that's the case. I was surprised all the same. I suspect Caranthir was actually training Philip to take on a bigger role at the hospital."

"Is that so?"

"Yes, but do keep that information to yourself, as I'm not certain. But I was in the break room only a couple of days before Philip was fired, and I overheard Philip and Caranthir talking in the next room. Philip was talking to Caranthir about invoicing and accounting. They were obviously keeping it hush-hush, so I just left. But I thought it was nice that Caranthir was helping Philip get a leg up on his career."

I stopped, my mouth dropping open. If anyone had chosen that exact moment to look at me, they definitely would have thought I'd seen a ghost. Everything clicked.

What was the name of that company on the invoices I'd gone through – Helio-something? Helios was the Greek god of the sun, and who had told me that Caranthir was the elvish name for Sun-God?

Plus, in his office, there had been a large picture of a sunrise.

I had a hunch that I knew exactly where Philip Vulcan had gotten all that money he spent. Where on earth were Amy and Sara?

I looked around once more, but couldn't spot them anywhere. I couldn't see Chief Enforcer King, either. Maybe she had gone home after speaking with Patricia.

I did, however, see Caranthir in the distance. He was walking down the path, away from the lake and back towards town, evidently having done enough grieving. Unfortunately, he was already way off in the distance, and I knew if I didn't take off after him now, there was no chance I would ever be able to catch up to him.

I shifted my weight from foot to foot, trying to decide what to do. After all, I probably shouldn't go after Caranthir alone. He was an elf, and I was just a witch who could do one spell, and I couldn't even do it that well. Not to mention, I was pretty sure he was a murderer.

On the other hand, my friends and law enforcement were nowhere to be seen. What if Caranthir decided that the heat was too heavy and he escaped? There would never be any justice for Myrtle, or even Patricia.

I knew what it was like to lose a loved one. I knew what it was like to be unable to get any justice, because unfortunately, cancer and heart disease weren't the sort of things you could get revenge on.

As the pain of losing my parents rose up in my chest once more, I knew what I was going to do. It might not have been the right decision, but it was the one I was making.

I started to run after Caranthir, checking one last time as I made my way past the people crowded around the tables to see if I could spot Amy or Sara, or Chief Enforcer King.

Nope. They weren't there; I was on my own.

CHAPTER 22

"Caranthir," I called out when I was only about thirty feet from the elf. We were definitely far from the lake now, and as I looked around and realized I could no longer see anybody in any direction, I started to think that maybe this was a bad idea.

"Oh, hello there, young witch. You're Tina, are you not? You're the new arrival in town."

I nodded. "Yeah, that's me."

"What can I do for you on this fine morning? It's nice to see you at a coven event, while Philip's death was sad, it really was a lovely service."

My goodness was this elf ever wordy.

"Absolutely, I was honored to have been a part of it." Yeah, this was a bad idea. I decided to backtrack on my plan to confront Caranthir. I was going to go back, speak with Amy, Ellie, and Sara about it, and then we could tell Chief Enforcer King what we had discovered and let her deal with it. That was definitely the much smarter play. "Sorry for interrupting. I just saw you leaving, and I wanted to say hi."

Caranthir smiled, and a wave of relief washed over me.

"Of course you were. Now, why don't you tell me why you were really here?"

That wave of relief quickly changed into one of pure dread.

"What do you mean?"

"You must not know much about elves. We have very good intuition."

Right. I'd literally *just* had this conversation with Kyran, like ten minutes earlier. Of course Caranthir could sense that I wasn't here just to make idle chit-chat.

"I don't know what you mean." Might as well double down on the lie. What did I have to lose, after all?

This time, Caranthir's smile didn't reach his eyes. "Of course you do. You think I killed Philip Vulcan. And I can't deny it, in fact, it is the truth. I am his murderer."

"You were embezzling from the hospital, and he found out," I said, trying out my theory, and Caranthir nodded solemnly.

"Yes, that is correct. I incorporated a company, Heliosupplies Limited, in one of the larger paranormal towns, where I knew I could get around undetected. I would then invoice that company for false services rendered."

"Helios being the Greek god of the sun," I said, nodding.

"I did not think anyone would make the connection if they ever had found out. However, I also hadn't expected a new arrival from the human world, and I certainly wasn't aware that you had discovered the invoices, only that you were investigating the murder and had spoken with Patricia multiple times."

"We broke into your offices to find out why Philip had been fired. We saw that you wrote he was fired, but Patricia Trovao swore that Philip never would have stolen anything."

Caranthir laughed, but the sound was cold and jarring. "Of course, she would think that. She was sleeping with him, wasn't she? I don't know if Philip ever stole anything, but the man certainly wasn't beyond threatening my good self with blackmail."

"That was why he had a ton of cash at the bar that night," I said.

"That is the case, yes. I allowed him to believe that I would pay him, although I was well aware that once the handouts began, they never would cease. Therefore, that night, after giving him a few hours to spend his money, I called him and asked him to meet me at The Magic Mule. I had no idea that was where he had spent his evening, as I, being an elf, do not frequent such lowly establishments as the local public house, and I certainly would never be seen at the one frequented by witches and wizards. Therefore, it was the perfect place to commit a murder; Chief Enforcer King would automatically assume the crime was committed by a witch or wizard, and given the man's propensity to follow his – erm, how to put it delicately – second brain, I assumed there would be no lack of suspects to be found among his own kind."

I resisted the strong urge to roll my eyes. This guy was not only pompous and pretentious, but he also seemed to feel that elves were inherently superior to other paranormal beings.

"Yeah, well, it can't have been that perfect a crime if *I* managed to figure it out. I'm barely even a witch."

"Yes, that was an unexpected, and rather problematic occurrence," Caranthir replied.

I wasn't entirely sure what was going to happen next. After all, I had a feeling Caranthir wasn't going to be entirely down with handing himself in to Chief Enforcer King.

"So, where do we go from here?"

"Well, now the only thing left to do is to silence the person who figured out I was the killer."

Great. Why hadn't I thought to ask Kyran if elves had any special weaknesses?

I took a step back and looked around. Nope, there was still no one anywhere nearby. Maybe if I made a run for it I had a chance, but Caranthir had to be a foot taller than me; he'd catch me easily. It wasn't as though I was particularly athletic.

Still, if it came down to a fight, I was still going to lose.

Neither fight nor flight seemed like particularly good options right now, but flight seemed like the less bad one.

I turned on my heel and ran, hoping that the element of surprise might net me a few extra feet of distance. After all, all I needed was to run far enough to get into view of someone, anyone, and then I could call for help. That was all I needed, to see someone else.

Running blindly back in the general direction of the lake – I couldn't remember exactly which path I'd taken – I looked around, hoping someone, anyone, would pop up into view.

"Help!" I called all the same, hoping my voice would carry further than my eyes could see. It didn't take long before Carathir caught up to me, though. Ice ran through my veins as soon as I felt his hand gripping the fabric of my shirt.

"Help me!" I called out in one last, desperate attempt at rescue before he reached over and covered my mouth with his hand. I tried to bite it, but couldn't manage it.

"Come on, little witch, it's time to get rid of you once and for all," Caranthir growled in my ear, dragging me towards a large fountain about thirty feet away. It was at least forty feet wide, and made in the style of the Trevi Fountain in Rome, with Jupiter in the middle and other, presumably lesser celestial beings at his feet. That said, I definitely wasn't focusing on the beauty of the architecture so much as the large, deep pool in front of the statue to which I was currently being dragged.

"It will be such a tragedy," Caranthir said slowly. "The new witch in town drowned in a tragic accident, in the coven gardens, no less."

I glowered at Caranthir, unable to say anything, and he laughed that same cruel laugh once more. "This really is your own fault for sticking your nose where it doesn't belong, witch. I hope you enjoyed your foray into the paranormal world."

And with that, Caranthir plunged my head deep into the water. For a second I started to struggle, but then I began to feel calm, the same calmness I felt when I fell into the water in the backyard. I realized a second later what I had to do. Instead of fighting the water, I embraced it. I pushed off the edge of the fountain, diving deeper into the water, but out of Caranthir's grasp.

I came back up about ten feet away, completely soaked, standing in waist-deep water, and pulled out my wand. Caranthir laughed.

"You must be joking. Even that idiot dragon I sent to scare you accidentally knocked you off the broom this morning, that's how awful a witch you really are."

I held firm. After all, Caranthir was right. I knew

one spell, which was completely useless, and it wasn't even a good one.

Caranthir made to come into the fountain to get me, when all of a sudden a ball of black fur came flying out of nowhere.

"Hy-ahh!" Mr. Meowgi called out as he launched himself toward's Caranthir, claws out and ready.

"What-" Caranthir cried out in surprise, an instant before Mr. Meowgi landed, turning Caranthir's cry of surprise into one of pain.

"Get off me, you mongrel!" he shouted.

"Mr. Meowgi! Be careful!" I called out to my cat, surprised at how quickly I had formed a bond with him. I didn't want him to get hurt, no matter what.

"Don't worry, these claws are better than nunchucks," Mr. Meowgi replied. A second later, however, Caranthir grabbed Mr. Meowgi and tore my cat off his face, launching him at a nearby tree.

"NO!" I shouted, my voice a panicked squeal as my familiar dropped to the ground, letting out a small meowl. As I heard the sound of his pain, something in my brain snapped.

"*By the power of water, make this elf suffer,*" I said, without even realizing it. Pointing the wand at Caranthir, a wave of water flew from the end and enveloped Caranthir.

"What is this? It burns! It's burning!" I stood, watching in a combination of horror and surprise as Caranthir writhed in pain. Did *I* do that?

Then my focus turned to Mr. Meowgi. I ran out of the fountain, leaving Caranthir to his fate, and made my way to my familiar. I picked him up delicately, cradling him in my arms.

"Are you alright?" I whispered to him. "Mr. Meowgi, please be alright."

CHAPTER 23

*M*r. Meowgi opened his eyes slightly. "I am sorry. I failed you, sensei."

"No. No, you didn't fail me at all," I said, tears falling from my eyes. "You're amazing, Mr. Meowgi. You came to rescue me, and you're going to be ok. Now, let's get out of here."

As I got up, however, the tree against which Mr. Meowgi had been thrown began to uproot and fell to the ground. I turned to see Caranthir holding out a hand towards it. Right. Kyran had said elves had a very earth-based magic. His face was scratched red, and he looked like he was in horrible pain, but he was still not going to go down without a fight. With the tree blocking our path, we now had to get past him to escape. But how? I had no idea what the spell that I'd done even *was*, let alone how to do it again. It had just been, well, instinct when I'd seen Mr. Meowgi hurt.

And the only other spell I knew was actually useless here.

Still, I knew that no matter what, I had to get help for my kitty. No matter what it took.

Caranthir took a threatening step towards me. "Right, I'm going to get rid of both of you," he growled, and I stepped back, pressing against the trunk of the tree.

"Tina, duck!" I heard a familiar voice say, and I didn't even bother to look up. A second later a gust of wind passed above me, and I looked up to see Amy riding on the back of Sara's broom. She had her wand out, and a second later a magical bubble escaped from it and encapsulated Caranthir.

He pressed against it, but unlike the bubbles I made with soap as a kid, this one didn't pop. In fact, nothing happened at all. I could see his mouth moving inside of it, but couldn't hear anything.

The broom carrying my two friends swept around, and they landed next to me.

"Tina, are you alright?"

"I am, but I'm not sure if Mr. Meowgi is," I replied. "He's definitely hurt."

"Come with me," Sara said. "We'll take him to my mom."

"Do you guys not have vets here?" I asked as I climbed onto the broom and held onto Sara with one hand, carefully holding Mr. Meowgi with the other."

"What's a vet?" Sara asked.

"Chief Enforcer King is on her way," Amy said. "I'll make sure that Caranthir can't leave this particular prison until she gets here. You enjoy that, it's probably a nicer prison than where you're going," she said, glowering at the elf.

I didn't have to hear him to know he was swearing his head off at Amy. So much for mister cool, collected and super-pretentious.

But right now, I had more important things to take care of. "Ok, let's go," I said to Sara, and she lifted the broom off the ground once more.

With Sara in charge of the broom, the ride was fast, smooth, and didn't end with anyone falling off. She landed in front of the hospital a couple minutes later, and we burst through the emergency room doors.

"Mom!" Sara called out, waving a hand at her mother, whose mop of red hair stood out at the back of the room.

"Sara, what is it?" Heather Neach asked, coming over. "I'm quite busy today."

"It's Mr. Meowgi," I said, holding my cat out to her. "He was attacked. Please, fix him."

"Oh goodness, poor thing," Heather said instantly. "Bring him over here."

I raced over to the room Heather indicated, and placed him on the flat, stainless-steel table inside.

"Tell me he's going to be ok," I muttered, my hands moving to my mouth.

"It's going to take more than that elf to end me," Mr.

Meowgi muttered, and I almost started to cry. Still, I was hoping for an actual doctor to give me the ok instead.

Heather poked and prodded at Mr. Meowgi for a little bit, and as soon as she touched one of his ribs, he let out a howl of pain.

"I think I know what he has, let me do a spell to make sure."

Heather took out her wand and pointed it at Mr. Meowgi's side. A second later, an X-ray of my familiar appeared on the wall, as if projected there, and I gasped.

"Yes, that's a broken rib for sure," Heather nodded. "Just as I suspected. Let me get a potion made for him, and he'll be good as new in just a couple of minutes."

I patted Mr. Meowgi on the head gently while Heather left the room.

"Thank you for saving me," I whispered to him, tears now falling openly. "You were so brave."

"Like Bruce Lee?"

"Exactly like Bruce Lee

"And you," I said, turning to Sara. "Thank you. You saved us both."

Sara blushed heavily, obviously not used to such praise.

"I didn't do much, really. I just brought Amy over so she could do the actual spell."

"How did you know I was in trouble?"

"Mr. Meowgi. He came over and began acting crazy,

and we knew something was wrong. Amy and I ran to grab my broom, and then Amy did a spell to find you, and told me where to go. When we saw Caranthir looking like a crazy person, we figured he was attacking you, and so she stopped him. As soon as we landed Amy texted Chief Enforcer King and told her where we were."

"He's the one who killed Philip," I said. "I figured it out, and I couldn't see you and Amy anywhere, or Chief Enforcer King. I went to confront him, then decided it was a bad idea, but he already knew, and tried to kill me. Then Mr. Meowgi came and saved my life."

"I heard your cries for help," Mr. Meowgi said, his eyes still closed.

"How come you heard them, and not anyone else?"

"He's your familiar," Sara explained. "The two of you have a stronger bond than anyone else. He's much more sensitive to your cries than anyone else would be."

"Ah, that explains it," I said, nodding, just as Heather came back into the room. She carried in her hand a small cauldron; it was basically the size of a cereal bowl, but made of cast-iron instead of ceramics. The inside of the cauldron was half-filled with a deep, blue liquid. Its thick viscosity reminded me of mud, and as it bubbled away slowly, with a big bubble forming and popping every couple of seconds, I had to wonder exactly what it was.

Heather pulled out a syringe and filled it with some of the liquid, then made her way to Mr. Meowgi.

"Alright, little guy. Open wide," Heather said, and Mr. Meowgi happily lapped up the mixture. "Tastes like fish, delicious," he muttered. "Oooh, and my rib feels better, too."

"Just a little bit more," Heather said. "I'm not sure the dosage rate for cats, but hopefully it's similar to humans."

"Are there no vets in Western Woods?" I asked.

"Again, what's a vet?" Sara asked, cocking her head to the side.

"A veterinarian. Basically, a doctor who specializes in taking care of animals."

"No. If there's ever been an issue we just take them to the regular Healers," Sara replied. "That's an interesting concept, a Healer for pets."

"It certainly is," Heather said. "Now, Mr. Meowgi should be good as new in a few minutes. Would you like me to look you over as well, dear?" she continued, looking me over. "You look as though you've gotten yourself into a wee little bit of trouble, lately."

I shook my head and smiled. I *definitely* would have looked like a drowned rat, now. "No, thank you. Mr. Meowgi certainly needed your help a lot more than me. I only look like a disaster right now, I feel mostly fine."

"What did the two of you get into, anyway?"

Sara and I shared a look. "It's a very long story."

"Alright, well, you can take him home now."

"Good, and I feel like I deserve some fresh fish to help me recover from such a nasty fight," Mr. Meowgi said. "After all, I took on an elf who was much bigger than me, and I won."

Seeing as Mr. Meowgi had saved my life by doing so, I had to agree. "Alright," I smiled. "Sara will take us to the store and you can pick out the piece of fish you want yourself."

CHAPTER 24

*T*hat night, the four of us were sitting in the living room, enjoying a desert made up of brownies leftover from the café that Ellie had brought back home. They looked like ordinary brownies, except for the colorful rock-like substances that dotted the tops of them. When you bit into them, the rocks exploded, a little bit like pop rocks, giving the brownies a nice little extra oomph.

"That elf who works for The Magic Word – that's the local paper," Sara explained to me, "came by today. He wanted to interview me for a story." Her face blushed red with excitement. "He told me it's going to be in next week's edition. I can't wait to show my mom. She's finally going to see that just being good at the broom came in handy for once."

"That's great news," Ellie said, taking a big bite. "I

can't believe I missed all of the excitement, but I'm glad everyone's ok!"

Mr. Meowgi was currently recuperating in my bedroom, having decided that being the hero for the day meant he had earned the right to take up the entire bed.

"Me too," I said. "Thank you so much to all of you."

"Hey, what are friends for?" Amy asked. "Although I do wish you had found us before you confronted Caranthir."

"So do I," I laughed.

"Don't worry about Amy, she's just a bit salty because someone else solved a puzzle before she did," Ellie told me with a wink, earning a scowl from Amy.

"That's just not true. Besides, we didn't overhear the conversation that allowed Tina to put the puzzle pieces together."

"There it is, there's always an excuse when Amy's not the smartest person in a room," Sara laughed, and Amy stuck her tongue out at her.

"I'm quite happy that Caranthir is in prison, no matter who is responsible."

"Did he admit to everything?" I asked, and she nodded.

"Yes, when Chief Enforcer King got there he broke down completely, and admitted to everything. Chief Enforcer King says he's going to spend the rest of his life at the magical prison, Alakazam. He looked absolutely horrible, too. What did you do to him?"

As all eyes turned onto me, I gulped. I hadn't thought about the mystery spell in a few hours. "To be honest, I'm not sure." I explained to my new friends how I had dived into the pool, and how, when Mr. Meowgi hit the tree, that spell just... happened.

"Wow," Sara breathed when I finished. "That's crazy. I've never heard of anything like that happening before."

"It's very interesting," Amy nodded, looking at me closely. "I believe we can narrow down your coven to one guided by a celestial being of water."

"Are there a lot of those?"

"Mercury, Neptune, Pluto, the moon, Ceres, and Titan, just to name a few," Amy rattled off on her fingers. I sighed. Great. It felt like we'd barely narrowed it down at all. "Sorry, but water-influenced covens are among the most common," she continued. "But it's a start."

"So how come I knew a spell, just like that?" I asked.

"Well, it's interesting. The thing is, there have very rarely been any examples of witches who have come to the paranormal world as adults, so very few examples of witches who have gotten into a situation like yours who *didn't* know the spells. I can't think of anything I've read ever happening in a similar manner."

"That's Amy-code for she has no freaking clue," Ellie laughed. "I think it's instinct. I think somewhere in your witch brain, a spell from your coven came to you when you were both stressed, and surrounded by your ruling power's element."

"But… I've never known anything about my coven. I didn't even know which element my coven was linked to."

"Well, that's the instinct part. Maybe somewhere, deep down, you actually already know the spells, and all we're doing when learning them is bringing them back. Knowing Mr. Meowgi was in trouble, and surrounded by water, yours came to the fore."

I nodded. That made sense, actually, in a way. Maybe I really did know all this magic deep down, and in desperation, my brain managed to dig up a spell to help me that it didn't even know it knew.

We were suddenly interrupted by a knock at the front door.

"I'll get it," I said, jumping up. It was now getting late in the evening, and as I made my way towards the door, I realized how silly it was that I was the one getting it. No one that I knew was going to come by this late.

Sure enough, as I opened the door, I found myself staring at a man with short, blue-black hair, light brown eyes, and skin so pale it was almost white. He looked to be about my age, leaning casually against the side wall of the building.

"Hello," I said, wondering which of my roommates this guy was after.

"Hey. You're Tina, the new witch."

"Yes, that's me."

"Look. Jackson sent me here. I'm Jormund, the dragon who knocked you off your broom this morning."

"Oh." I didn't really know what else to say.

"I'm supposed to apologize to you."

"Well, it sounds super earnest so far."

Jormund sighed. "I seriously didn't mean to hurt you. Look, I told Jackson everything. Caranthir came up to me the other day – I work security at the hospital part-time – and asked me if I wanted to make some extra cash. I mean, yeah, who doesn't? So he told me I had to scare the new witch in town. When I saw you practicing on your broom, I thought I'd give you a bit of a fright. Do a fly-by, you know? I didn't expect you to actually be so new you'd fall off your broom."

"That was my first time ever on a broom."

"No kidding? Well, yeah. So I got paid, but when I saw you falling, I did feel really bad. I'm glad nothing happened to you, really."

"So you didn't do it because you thought I had killed Philip Vulcan?"

"Are you kidding? What do I care who killed that idiot? I'm not surprised it was Caranthir. He wouldn't tell me why he wanted you scared, just told me that if I wanted my money I'd do it, and I'd keep my mouth shut about it. But no, I didn't think you had killed Philip. I just did it for the cash, and I really didn't mean to knock you off your broom. I didn't realize that was going to happen. I hope we're cool."

I took a second, then nodded. "Thank you for the apology." Jormund kicked his foot into the ground, looking a bit awkward.

"Thanks. I, uh, know I screwed up. Thanks for being so nice about it. See you around, and welcome to town."

And with that, Jormund turned and left. I had to admit, I felt a fair bit of relief at his confession. It was actually a bit better to know that he had been hired to scare me off from investigating the murder rather than having done it because he thought I had killed Philip.

Making my way back into the living room, I told the girls what had happened. "What's going on with the new pool in our backyard, anyway?" I asked.

Ellie grinned. "We decided to keep it. After all, none of us ever really went into the backyard anyway, and this way we can relax out there with floaties."

"I cleaned it up a little bit," Amy added. "I made it six feet deep, and added a shallow end at one point, and tiles to make it nicer to walk along."

"That's amazing."

"And we never would have thought to turn it into a pool if you hadn't been knocked off your broom," Ellie said.

"Or if Sara's spell hadn't gone wrong and made the water to begin with," Amy added.

"It looks like Tina's arrival has already changed

things for the better," Sara laughed. "Welcome to Western Woods!"

First of all, I wanted to thank you for reading this book. I well and truly hope you enjoyed reading this book as much as I loved writing it.

If you enjoyed Back to Spell One I'd really appreciate it if you could take a moment and leave a review for the book on Amazon, to help other readers find the book as well.

Want to read more of Tina's adventures? The second book in the Western Woods Mystery series is now available!

Other Western Woods Mysteries

Two Peas in a Potion (Western Woods Mystery #2)

Three's a Coven (Western Woods Mystery #3)

Four Leaf Clovers (Western Woods Mystery #4)

Willow Bay Witches Mysteries

The Purr-fect Crime (Willow Bay Witches #1)

Barking up the Wrong Tree (Willow Bay Witches #2)

Just Horsing Around (Willow Bay Witches #3)

Lipstick on a Pig (Willow Bay Witches #4)

A Grizzly Discovery (Willow Bay Witches #5)

Sleeping with the Fishes (Willow Bay Witches #6)

Get your Ducks in a Row (Willow Bay Witches #7)

Busy as a Beaver (Willow Bay Witches #8)

Magical Bookshop Mysteries

Alice in Murderland (Magical Bookshop Mystery #1)

Murder on the Oregon Express (Magical Bookshop Mystery #2)

The Very Killer Caterpillar (Magical Bookshop Mystery #3)

Death Quixote (Magical Bookshop Mystery #4)

Pride and Premeditation (Magical Bookshop Mystery #5)

Moonlight Cove Mysteries

Witching Aint's Easy (Moonlight Cove Mystery #1)

Witching for the Best (Moonlight Cove Mystery #2)

Thank your Lucky Spells (Moonlight Cove Mystery #3)

A Perfect Spell (Moonlight Cove Mystery #4)

California Witching Mysteries

Witches and Wine (California Witching Mystery #1)

Poison and Pinot (California Witching Mystery #2)

Merlot and Murder (California Witching Mystery #3)

Cassie Coburn Mysteries

Poison in Paddington (Cassie Coburn Mystery #1)

Bombing in Belgravia (Cassie Coburn Mystery #2)

Whacked in Whitechapel (Cassie Coburn Mystery #3)

Strangled in Soho (Cassie Coburn Mystery #4)

Stabbed in Shoreditch (Cassie Coburn Mystery #5)

Killed in King's Cross (Cassie Coburn Mystery #6)

Ruby Bay Mysteries

Death Down Under (Ruby Bay Mystery #1)

Arson in Australia (Ruby Bay Mystery #2)

The Killer Kangaroo (Ruby Bay Mystery #3)

ABOUT THE AUTHOR

Samantha Silver lives in British Columbia, Canada, along with her husband and a little old doggie named Terra. She loves animals, skiing and of course, writing cozy mysteries.

You can connect with Samantha online on Facebook.

Printed in Great Britain
by Amazon